I0742534

My Dog, Me

Novel

Anthony Schlagel

Wet Cement Press
Berkeley, California

Thank you Lucy Ellmann,
for your hawk-eyed and kind editing help.

Copyright© 2019 Anthony Schlagel
All rights reserved

ISBN: 978-1-7324369-3-0

Wet Cement Press
Berkeley, California

www.wetcementpress.com
wetcementpress@gmail.com

Cover Illustration:
"Head of Snarling Dog from Life, by Mr.
Wood." Appeared in *The Descent of Man*,
Charles Darwin, 1871.

Contents

One foot in the door
The other foot in the gutter
The sweet smell that they adore
I think I'd rather smother

　—*The Replacements*

I Stood Beside My Bike In Anger

The door opened and the reek of cooked cabbage, cigarette smoke, and premature old age gushed out. She handed me the key without touching my hand, pulled her robe aside to show me her swollen, purple leg, and told me to go upstairs alone. I was about to stick the key in the hole when I noticed a note jabbed over a nail at eye level.

> Darla Fuck you
> you are a Cunt
> I don't Ever Want to See You agin

I pulled the note off, folded it neatly and put it in my back pocket. I'm a collector of messages meant for other people. Intimate letters are the best kind, found on sidewalks or in waste baskets. It was my first that year. I went inside.

The smell of vacancy and a layer of dust greeted me. The apartment hadn't been lived in for months. A single bed up by the ceiling, a blue ladder made out of two-by-fours leading up to it. In the next room, a rusty-legged 1950s-era Formica table with faded, ripped vinyl chairs. In the kitchen, pots and pans on plywood boards screwed into the wall. I opened a drawer, picked up a bent fork that'd been stuck into a lot of rotten-toothed mouths over the years.

The orange couch sagged and I sprang up. I went into the bathroom. The stink of mold. Four inches of green water in the shower. Back in the living room I pulled the French window up from the floor and it gave no resistance. I stepped onto the balcony. I bent down and felt the rivets in the tin floor to make sure they were flush. A big leafy shade tree dappled the sun. I jumped up to look over the plywood partition that split the balcony in half. Nobody over there.

I jumped again. No furniture, nothing. Just a half-dead potted plant. Was it safe to think I had no neighbor? I smelled decaying plants. A storm cloud was about to burst. I leapt downstairs, taking three at a time.

A Camel dangled out of the corner of the caretaker lady's decomposing mouth. When was the last time it'd been kissed, and how drunk had the kisser been? I gave her forty dollars and didn't sign a piece of paper. She breathed hard and asked no questions. I told her I'd be back in thirty minutes with my stuff and the rest of the money. She didn't shake my hand or touch me. I liked her.

On Magazine Street I felt refreshed. A pile of fresh dog shit made me change my stride. I unchained my bike, hopped on and pedaled toward the youth hostel. Rain began falling warmly. I was happy. I'd found my place.

A dog leapt out, snarling and barking, but an iron gate kept him back a foot, so I told the dog to fuck off. He kept snarling and barking, so I straddled my bike like I was going to kick him in the face. Rain fell soft and lovely.

No one was at the front desk of the youth hostel. The big room I shared with ten men from Europe was empty, but still stank of ten men sharing a shower room and two toilets. I stuffed my things into my backpack and thought of what I might steal. I'd had a camera stolen from me in a youth hostel once.

The front desk phone rang, and was still ringing when I walked by. I waited. I wanted to say goodbye to the guy from Siberia who worked there. He was nice and easy to talk to. The phone rang until it stopped, then I went outside.

I rode unsteadily. Two boys in about sixth grade laughed and pointed at me. Did I look funny? The sun came out hot. The bushes steamed and gleamed. The same dog as before jumped out at me but this time I didn't react.

My clothes were soaked with rain and sweat as I handed the caretaker lady the cash. $150 a month, you couldn't beat that. A little white dog appeared at her side. It yapped like a baby guard dog.

I said, "I didn't know you had a dog."

I said, "Does it bark?"

"What?"

I said, "Does it bark a lot? The dog."

Maybe it would have been different if I'd had a dog, but I didn't.

"It depends on what you mean by a lot."

She didn't smile. I didn't like her. I lugged my backpack up the stairs. I went back down for the bike. I shut the door behind me. Home was having a door to close and lock behind me. I took my clothes off and went out to the warm tin-floored balcony and had sex with myself. I'm being frank. The sun dappled by the shade tree struck my face. I closed my eyes.

I opened my eyes and took a shower in the green water that came up to my ankles. I went back out to the balcony and sun-dried with no fear of being seen. The tops of people's heads walking on the sidewalk were at an extreme angle. I went back into the apartment to look around. I climbed the blue ladder and lay down on the narrow bed. My ass pulsated wet into the mattress.

The air was stifling. Who in fuck's name had lofted a bed three feet from the ceiling in New Orleans? And it was only April.

The bed sheet stank of stale pussy juice, sweat and come. My asshole itched, like something small with many legs had crawled up inside it. The sheet was gray, not white anymore. The bed was narrow. If I turned over, I would have fallen eight feet down to the floor.

"What kind of person writes a note, and punches it over a nail?"

"An angry man," I answered.

"An angry, somewhat illiterate man."

"Yes, he did spell 'again' 'agin.' But who are you to judge?"

"I'm no one to judge."

The guy had channeled his rage into a note and poked it through a nail, god bless him. It was better than punching Darla. I could never have written a note like that. I wasn't able to project on a level that great. I blamed Colette for everything, but I also knew I was half to blame, so I restrained myself. I'd been raised to be nice, in a nice suburb of Milwaukee. I'd boarded an airplane with money in my pocket, and flown away, all so I wouldn't poke a note through Colette's nail.

The note jabber, though, was capable of projecting rage at incredibly close range. To his credit, though, he'd turned his rage into writing. He'd even "posted" it. Then, like a man, he'd gone to some local watering hole to cool off.

I was lying on Darla's bed, my wet ass sweating into it. Would the note poker be back? Did he have a spare key? Was he on his way back right now? Would he storm in and stab me through the bottom of the bed with a butcher knife? I didn't want to be a cripple, so I climbed down the blue ladder and put my clothes on.

Darla was black, and the angry man was black. I presumed this because most of the neighborhood was black. I was white. The caretaker lady was white. The boys who'd pointed and laughed at me were white and black. But being poor, whatever color you are, makes it probable that you have to stick around the neighborhood.

Darla took a bus to Baton Rouge to stay with her sister. It had to be done. I had to get her out of town. But where was there for *him* to go? I had him storm down into his brother's basement, three blocks away, where he was begging himself to go back right now and give it to Darla good.

There would be a knock on the door any second. I would play possum. It would happen fast. The door would be kicked in. He would shout, "Who the fuck are you?" I would say, "I just moved in, I don't know!" He would say, "Have you been fucking Darla?" I would say, "I don't even know Darla!" Then there would be a moment of silence. Then we would both eye the kitchen, and race to the drawer to see who could get to the bent knives first.

I ran water in the bathroom sink for a long time but it didn't get cold. I brushed my teeth. I paced the scuffed, warped wooden floor. Black people were complicated. They had complicated passions I didn't understand. I didn't know anything about black people. I went down to the lobby to look at the mailbox to see whose name was on it.

Darla Thompson.

I knocked on the caretaker lady's door to get my mailbox key. I could hear the television. She was playing possum. I hated people who played possum. I knocked harder. Nothing. I went and stood in the front doorway of the building. I thought of writing Colette a long detailed letter explaining how I was feeling about Darla.

I went back up to my balcony to look at dusk coming on. My problems weren't behind me. I hadn't outsmarted anything. I hadn't escaped. It'd taken me five days to find a place, and I'd found it, and now things weren't different.

I needed to take a nap, but I didn't want to because I wanted to sleep later. I picked my bike up and carried it into the hallway. I listened in front of the other upstairs door. I held my breath and listened. I carried my bike downstairs. I listened at the door on the first floor across from the caretaker lady. Were we the only ones living there?

I was about to knock on her door and ask, "Are we the only ones living here?" but I didn't. I pushed the bike outside, put my left foot in the stirrup, hopped on, swung my right leg over the tube, and rode off.

The houses and apartments were ramshackle, not nice. I turned the corner and there were mansions, grand and set back from the street, lawns as big as apartment buildings, neatly trimmed hedges and bushes, tall leafy shade trees that were older than the Civil War.

I dropped my bike on the sidewalk and put my whole face into a Magnolia blossom. My suffering ended. I pulled my face back out, my suffering came back. I put my face back in. A couple, a man and a woman, white, approached on foot, talking in low, secretive voices so I quickly pulled my face back out.

I thought of the other note I had folded up in my back pocket. The phone number of my best friend's girlfriend's sister. I'd been told to call her once I got into town. And I would, when I was ready. I patted my back pocket to make sure it was there.

When the approaching couple was past me they raised their voices back up to a normal level. Was what they were saying so important and personal? I turned around and gave them the finger. They weren't looking.

I picked my bike up and rode to the gentle hum of air conditioners in the pastel dark Garden District. A man approached on foot, white arms swinging. He was speed-walking. How ridiculous. I wanted to turn around and pedal up his ass.

The houses changed. I wasn't in the Garden District anymore. The houses were small and falling over, even caving in. Poor people lived in them. Black people were spilling out, hanging around the fronts of the buildings. Dozens of them. The yards were small, the grass burnt by the sun or trampled by feet.

Black girls jumped rope. Black boys shot hoops on portable baskets on both sides of the street. I rode around them, afraid they might fast break through me. Little kids kicked rocks and cans. I wove in and out. A girl, about five years old, ran alongside me laughing. She grabbed my bike seat. A woman shouted from an upper-story window, "Leave him be, Jackie!"

I was the only white person around, sailing through on quiet rubber wheels. I smelled meat grilling—chicken, beef, pork, fish—all the meats. I went around the corner, did a u-turn, and rode back to the Garden District to find a place to eat.

Cicadas, crickets, and frogs sang full-throated. There weren't so many humans in large groups in front of ugly edifices. What a difference an inheritance of a few hundred thousand dollars can make. I heard a woman laughing. Was she laughing at me? Did I look funny?

A white woman, laughing and talking on a cell phone, pushing a baby stroller, was coming at me on the left side of the sidewalk. I held my ground, and was prepared to plow into her. Generosity has its limits. At the last second I swerved. Who can run into a baby? The mother never saw me.

I heard voices and saw a swinging wooden sign. "Late Nite Happy Hour 9 to 11." A garden set behind a hedge trimmed flat. The voices formed a hum. From the sidewalk I squinted, saw lit candles on tables, and was jealous. They were happy. I didn't belong in the white neighborhood anymore than I belonged in the black neighborhood. I felt in my back pocket for my best friend's girlfriend's sister's phone number. I wanted to call, but I didn't want a connection that might lead to a demand. I rode home.

There were no distractions in the apartment. It was going to be a hard night. No neighbors at least, and no cell phone to call Colette with because I'd smashed it, again and again, against a cement-block airport bathroom wall.

I heard the door creak. I jumped up, made a fist, ready to punch. I opened the door. Nobody there. I went to the bathroom, ran lukewarm water over my wrists. A farmer told me once that running water over your wrists is a good way to stay hydrated. I looked for a towel, no towel. Not in the bathroom, not in the kitchen. Furnished apartment, my ass! I paced the warped floor.

Short of putting food in my mouth I had nothing to do. Too dim to read, and I didn't have a book. I'd moved into a dump, a hole, a place where people go who can't afford to live. I looked at the clock on the wall in the kitchen, but there wasn't a clock on the wall in the kitchen. I swore there'd been one.

I stepped out onto the tin floor of the balcony. It was cool and my feet liked it. Another cloud burst and I took my shirt off. The street was busy with people running and the hissing of car tires. I took my pants off, and did fifty jumping jacks and peeked over the top of the plywood partition to see if anybody lived over there.

The plywood was nailed into a wooden Greek column on one end, and on the other end it was nailed into the siding of the house. The nails on both ends were bent. I swung around the column to have a better look. It was rotten and paint-chipped, and it left white chalk in my hands. I wiped them on my wet thighs.

If the caretaker's little dog was barking, it was out of range. I sat down on the tin floor, my back to the siding. I took my notebook out to make a list of things to buy: soap, shampoo, towel, sheets. I went into the kitchen to add to the list: a cup, coffee filters, coffee, bread, butter. I went back out to the balcony. A street-light had come on. I covered my eyes. It was ten feet away. If I leaned just right, at an awkward angle, the tree blotted it out. Add to the list: reading lamp.

I heard someone walking by on the side-walk, left to right. A man going somewhere. I was a man already there. And already I needed to get out. Cars were whizzing past. Magazine Street was busier than I'd thought it would be. Headlights flashed past. More cars, like a wave. Then no cars. I stood up to study this.

I looked to the right, down the street. A traffic light was stopping cars in a huddle, then releasing them like dogs at the start of a race. I could hear cicadas, crickets and frogs. Then another wave. I pointed my finger at the lead car and shot it dead.

I heard a noise coming from a bush below. Cat? Dog? Possum? Skunk? Raccoon? I bent over the railing to look. An insect dropped on my neck and I brushed it off, and kicked it away. I hoped I didn't kill it. Then more bugs fell and crawled on me. Bugs were everywhere. I ran to get a shoe. I put my hand in the shoe and stomped them dead by the hundreds. Too many to care about, too many to kill.

I looked for a broom to sweep away the dead. No broom. Not even a broom closet. I was about to march down to the caretaker lady and demand *broom*, but I was hot and hungry, and a little light-headed.

I went to slam the French window shut. It boomed. I held my breath and waited for a downstairs neighbor to yell. I lay down on the slanted floor and panted. I had to eat something. I slapped my face and a cockroach flew off. I'd never seen a flying cockroach before. I'd never seen a cockroach before.

I'd been taught that animals were made by God to be rounded up and eaten, employed, or generally unnoticed. The animals I'd known growing up were weak: Cows, pigs, chickens, dogs, cats, houseflies. Cockroaches, with their doctrine of inheriting the earth, had rebellion in their hearts.

I went to the balcony. Fresh air. A pack of cars hissing by. Then a yelp. "Yelp! Yelp! Yelp!"—each yelp weaker, then nothing.

I crouched, looked through the railing and the leaves to see. To the right, a few houses down, a black dog lay on the dark street. It looked like a punctured tire. A new wave of cars was coming.

I jammed one leg into my pants and fell over. It was dead, what could I do? I stood up, put the other leg in. Headlights were veering around it. A car caught the dog and dragged it until it landed right under me. I put my shirt on, buttoned it up crooked.

A black dog running loose at night.

A shadow came out from the other side of the street. It walked up to the dog and knelt down like a doctor. Cars came. It stood up like a policeman and directed cars around the dog. It knelt back down.

A shadow came out from my side of the street, right out from under me. It passed through the streetlight. I saw that it was a white boy with no shirt on.

The two shadows met, picked the dog up, and carried it across the street to the far side. They passed through a streetlight on that side.

I saw that the first shadow was a black man, and the dog's head dangled backward and to the side like a dead Civil War soldier.

I wanted to call Colette to tell her everything. How sad and forgiving I could be. How I'd been about to go down and do something. But Colette was engaged to be married, and I wasn't allowed to tell her anything.

But I'd thought I was going to tell her everything. How life was a virus. How we were nothing but maggots crawling on a carcass. How pigs have babies but they have enough dignity not to get carried away with their self-importance and make a PBS documentary called "The Miracle of Life"!

I had to get away.

I carried my bike down the stairs and rode back to the "Late Nite Happy Hour 9 to 11" sign. Citronella torches burned along the walkway. The patio was populated by tropical flowering plants. Low laughter, quiet conversation. Men tall and well-trimmed. Women clean and self-confident. Perfume mingled with cigar stench. Men with ties still tied on tight, like they enjoyed being strangled. I was wearing cut-off blue jeans and a dirty white shirt that had "One Shot Junior" on the front.

In my cab in Milwaukee I'd picked up this guy who was wearing a shirt with "One Shot Junior" on it, so I asked him what it meant. He said he was in a band that originally was called "I Shot JR"—as in *Dallas*, the TV show—but the kids who read the name on telephone posts and bulletin boards thought it was "One Shot Junior" (they were too young to have seen *Dallas*) so the band changed its name to "One Shot Junior."

I focused on the prettiest woman on the patio. I watched her every move. She came walking toward me. She wore a short skirt and had athletic thighs. Her breasts were tanned but white near the top of her low-slung top.

I smiled to see if I was good-looking. Her eyes glanced off me. She learned what she already knew—that *she* was beautiful. I finished my beer and left.

I hopped on my bike and moseyed down the street. I undulated from curb to curb. I came to a cemetery. The gate was open so I rode in. Japanese tourists on a ghost tour with lots of cameras around their necks were listening to a woman in a black 19th century dress. Spooky giggling came from behind a tombstone. I rode past, and out the opposite gate. A tour bus was idling, and the driver, a heavy-set black man, was sitting in a wheel-well eating some kind of sandwich.

"Hello," I said.

He ignored me.

Was it my fault I grew up in Wisconsin, and was raised without a prejudiced bone in my body?

A dog came running down the sidewalk, its owner jogging a hundred feet behind. I shouted, "Put your dog on a leash!" But it was just a collie, tame and nice, that wanted to be petted.

Shade trees made a tall tunnel over the street. High streetlights were covered by moss and leaves that made the street dim and sweet. I wondered what the trees were like back in the black neighborhood. Had there been trees? I rode back to find out.

I came to a tall apartment building built in the 1970s, ugly as a dungeon. Half the windows were open, the other half had loud, clanging, dripping air conditioners hanging off them. No balconies. A monstrosity. I stood beside my bike in anger.

A fenced-in yard ran parallel to the side-walk, long and narrow with a gate in front so people could be funneled in and out. But the people had pulled the gate off its hinges and trampled the fence so they could come and go as they pleased.

People sat on lawn chairs, stood, or milled around. They lived in heated boxes so they were outside shouting, talking and laughing. Cans of beer and candy wrappers, pieces of tin foil littered the dirt. The air was still, hot and humid. I needed to talk to somebody, so I pulled my bike over to a group of men who were standing around. They stopped talking.

"Weed?"

"Coke? Crack? Crank?"

"What you want then?"

"I don't want to buy anything. I just want to talk."

They burst out laughing. I got back on my bike and rode away. I could hear them laughing behind me. A rock sailed past my head. But I didn't have anything to do with slavery. My people came from France and Finland in the late 1800s. I had nothing to do with it.

I'd forgotten to look at the trees. I stopped at the corner store, bought a box of Red Beans and Rice for a dollar fifty.

The caretaker lady's stink came out from under the door. Did she do anything but smoke, eat cabbage, not pick up her dog's shit, and avoid bathing? I heard TV noises, and envisioned her dog curled up in her lap like a fold of her own flesh. "TV die!" I said, as I lugged my bike up the stairs quietly, listening for sounds at the other doors.

I entered my shithole, found a frying pan, put water on to boil, put red beans and rice in the boiling water. It was past midnight. I found a plate. Scabs of Darla's old food were stuck on it. I scraped the scabs off with my fingernail, then went to the bathroom to wash my hands. Note: buy soap.

I counted my money.

When the red beans and rice were cooked I loaded up the plate and went out to the balcony. I took my shoes off. The tin floor felt cool on my toes. I ate fast and went back for more. A cockroach was walking across the frying pan. I grabbed the plastic grocery bag

19

and used it as a glove to scoop it up, careful not to squash it, and carried it to the balcony where I dropped it off the ledge, and went back in.

A different cockroach was walking in my red beans and rice. I pinched this one dead, using the plastic bag as a pliers. It crunched. I flushed it down the toilet and went back to the kitchen. No garbage pail. I flushed the red beans and rice down the toilet too.

I walked back to the corner store, bought two Hostess Twinkies and a can of Coke. The owner was from Iraq, Iran, Syria, Egypt, Palestine, or some other country, but mostly he was sleepy. A million insects were beating themselves to death against the streetlight high on the corner, and many millions more had fallen down to their deaths on the sidewalk below. I sidestepped them.

I threw the empty can of Coke into the bush under my balcony. I was tired and would pick it up in the morning. I ate the Hostess Twinkies while walking up the stairs, then there was nothing left to do.

The streetlight was in my face. Add to list: heavy curtains. I climbed up the blue ladder to the bed by the ceiling. Too fucking hot. I tried opening the window under the bed, but it was stuck. I climbed back up the blue ladder to give the window a tug from above, but it was stuck. I lay down on Darla's mattress. I turned onto my stomach. I smelled her breath. I turned over onto my back.

Men had come on Darla's face on the pillow. I sat up fast and scraped my forehead against the ceiling. I had to sleep! I threw the mattress down on the floor and it thumped. I listened for a neighbor to complain. I tiptoed to the window under the bed. I tried to open it again.

"Damn it, Darla! You took the curtain! And the garbage can! And the reading lamp! And the towels! And the broom! Because you knew the caretaker lady had a swollen purple leg and wouldn't check on you!"

I tried to forgive Darla.

She didn't steal the curtain and the rest of the stuff. Other people had, before she moved in. Darla had learned to live without them. She'd gotten used to the situation. She was the type of person who didn't need curtains. She liked big city noises. She needed the glare of a streetlight to fall asleep. She had to have the TV or radio on blaring to fall asleep.

If only I were more like Darla.

I tried to think of all the people who'd ever lived in the apartment. Hundreds had come and gone and left no trace. Each had believed in the apartment as their own, in their time, and now I believed in it too. This was interesting—for about five minutes.

I dragged the mattress outside to the balcony where it was cool, but insects dropped down. I pushed the mattress back inside. I lay down on the couch, but it sagged and my back hurt. I dragged the mattress outside. Insects fell. I slapped as many as I could to death. I was stubborn. I needed to defeat them all. I expected the ones who saw the carnage to run back to the rear and tell their friends to call off the attack.

I pushed the mattress inside. I slammed the French window down. I listened for neighbors. I lifted the French window up an inch, and laid the mattress down near the bottom for fresh air. An insect crawled up my nose. A walk-in refrigerator, big enough to sleep in, was what I needed.

I shouted at the pillow. I shouted at the floor. I heard cars driving by. People were going to work already? I went to the balcony to look for the dead dog. It was still there, on the curb under the streetlight.

I dragged the mattress back into the bedroom, grinding dirt, lint, dead skin, and bug guts into the floor. I noticed something I hadn't seen before. Right in front of me, a door. Between the bedroom and living room.

I lifted up the French window, closed the newfound door in the middle of the apartment all but a quarter of an inch, laid the mattress down, and put my nose and mouth right up to the crack. This way I could breath (kind of), and was shielded from bugs (kind of).

Buy a Bike New Orleans

I was sleeping with a woman I didn't know. I jumped out of bed, ran to turn the light on. She was gone. I went into the room with the couch. She wasn't in there either. I opened the door, looked down the hallway. When my head touched the pillow I knew there hadn't been a woman.

Cars were driving down Magazine Street at a fast clip. It was Friday morning. People were in a hurry to get where they didn't want to be for nine hours. I turned over and went back to sleep.

I woke up at eleven when I thought of coffee. I put my clothes on and walked my bike to the other door upstairs and listened. I walked downstairs and listened.

It was hot. I was sweating. I unbuttoned my shirt. The breeze felt good. I wanted to find a coffeehouse where I could feel comfortable sitting for hours.

I didn't ride to the French Quarter. I didn't want to go in that direction. I rode Uptown, to the area around Tulane University.

I found a place that was too bright. I found a place that was too small. I found a place that was too crowded. I found a place that was too privileged. I found a place that wasn't crowded but it was indoor-only.

After an hour of hunting I found PJ's on Maple Street. Sweet, big back patio. I tied my bike up to a parking meter. The cold air gave me goosebumps. I waited in line. I ordered a cup of hot coffee and a bear claw. I went to the back patio. The air was hot and heavy. I went back in for a napkin. Goosebumps. I went back out. Steaming hot.

Air conditioning is an asshole that teaches us that there is a mechanical difference between inside and outside. Shade, on the other hand, is a natural form, and it should make all the difference.

I sat at a table cut in two by shade. That way I could adjust my preference as the sun moved. My dirty white t-shirt didn't match the rubber-coated white chair and table. My right arm in the sun had sweat beads on it, my left arm in the shade didn't. I took my notebook out and subtracted the coffee and bear claw from the money I had. A *Times-Picayune* sports page lay trapped against the leg of a neighbor's chair. I went to retrieve it. I begged the pardon of the pair of legs above it.

I noticed a pair of legs joining another pair of legs. The heads joined. The heads bobbed up and down, side to side in patterns that I recognized. I sipped hot coffee and sweated. I took my notebook out. I had the idea to write a guidebook called *Buy a Bike New Orleans* that would revolutionize travel writing. I wrote: "Fly to a city you've never been to, buy a bike, ride around, rent a shithole apartment, and when the last month's rent is due refuse to pay it!"

My guidebook would sweep the nation. I'd make millions. No other book was like it. It'd appeal to young travelers who couldn't afford to travel, or who hated vacations. I wrote: "Visit poor minority neighborhoods, sneak into wealthy beach compounds, go where no tourist has felt comfortable going before!"

Many readers, in turn, would write their own book. And each book would refer back to my book, so I would cash-in forever. *Buy a Bike Bangkok, Buy a Bike Boston.* Maybe even *Buy a Bike Milwaukee.*

I sucked my pen and thought of product tie-ins. Air pumps, headlights, spokes, rims. I thought of buying property in Italy, Manhattan, or even Door County. I'd need to learn to swim because of all the swimming pools. I'd need to hire servants from whatever minorities lived in the area.

A man joined two women sitting at a table. He told jokes and punch lines like he was acting in a TV sitcom. Every few minutes a joke ignited and the women laughed. They loved his verbal tomfoolery.

I concentrated on my book. A woman said she loved a certain toy as a child. She wondered if she would be able to find it on eBay. I closed my eyes but her voice scraped over me like gravel. My lungs rose and fell. I opened my eyes. The young women were laughing at another something the sit-com actor had said.

I found a different table, in a corner under an isolated tree. No chair. I had to ask if I could use an extra chair. The couple I interrupted nodded their heads, like what I said, or did with my life was no concern of theirs.

I carried the chair back, careful not to scrape the bricks. I felt like an almond croissant.

The air conditioning shocked me. The barista had a sailor saluting a dolphin tattooed on her right bicep. A graduate student, resting his elbows on a stack of books, talked on his cell phone. "That's a bummer, man. What?

Huh? You're breaking up. Kickball at seven?"

I dusted croissant crumbs off my lap and adjusted my chair. I counted eighteen people on the patio—ten women, eight men. I had to piss. I took my shoulder bag and went back inside. I waited in line for the unisex toilet in a small blue-painted storage room. Dozens of iced coffee makers dripping, the smell sweet and sticky. I pissed and went out to the boiling street.

A senior citizen woman was waiting for the light to change. She saw me and clutched her purse. When the light changed, she took mincing steps across the street. I biked up close behind her. She gripped her purse tighter. I laughed and zipped past.

The sun was high and hot. There was nothing to do. Nobody knew me. I wanted to sleep. John Lennon loved to sleep more than any other Beatle. I read that. To the point that he missed important recording sessions. Bed, nest, and sleep were some of John's and my favorite words.

I stepped back into the apartment. Three photographs lay scattered on the floor. They must have fallen out when I threw the mattress down. I picked them up.

In one, a black man dressed in a cheap brown suit was smiling for the person holding the camera while he stood on the balcony. In another, a black man dressed in blue jeans and not wearing a shirt was standing by the stove sipping something from a wooden spoon and smiling for the camera. In the third, a black man dressed in dirty work clothes was standing in front of the apartment near the bush where I'd thrown the can of Coke, and he was smiling too.

They all looked happy and carefree, maybe even in love. But nobody snaps a photo of a miserable man, or a pissed-off man, or a man in the act of revenge. You can't trust a photograph, everybody knows that. But I looked at them for clues. I examined them to see how their arms hung. I looked at their smiles to gauge if they were authentic smiles. I looked for how the light of New Orleans fell on their faces. I looked for pots and pans I could recognize.

Darla had loved each of these men in turn, then she'd discarded them. Or they had discarded her. Their love affairs had started strong, but ended wrong. One of the men had stabbed a note over Darla's nail—which one?

Colette said, "Stop it, Nick!"

I said, "Colette, you fucked me over. I didn't fuck you over. Get out of here and stop judging me!"

I had Darla put a restraining order on the soiled man standing outside. But he didn't believe in the power of the government to restrain his whereabouts. He loved Darla, that was all he knew. He had nothing else—no job, no money, no education, no future. He loved Darla, so when Darla said "Enough!" he felt fucked over. I got it. A restraining order was just a test designed by Darla to see if he had the guts to break through it.

"I'll get a restraining order against you!" said Colette.

I couldn't believe she was still there. How dare she interrupt me. I'd gone away, hadn't I? Hadn't I left her alone? Hadn't I flown all the way down to New Orleans, where I'd never been, and didn't know anybody?

I had Darla call the cops to have him arrested. He took off. Two donut-dusted cops came by. One yawned and said, "If I were you, Missy, I'd get out of Dodge." The other cop wrote something down in a little notebook, then they left. Then Darla's boyfriend came back. Darla was desperate. He was desperate. They wanted love to last, finally. So they fucked, and it involved bruises and the best sex of their lives. In the morning, Darla called her sister, a tweaker in Baton Rouge. She took a bus to the Greyhound station. Her sister was nuts. From the frying pan into the fire. At last the Greyhound bus came.

Handsome men. Sunny pictures.

Colette was more than a sweet face. She had a body that was hard and soft, and strong and sexy. She walked with a loose gait. But I threw away the photographs I had of her. Burned them, actually. The smell her body gave off was of chemicals. Photographs of bodies are nothing but chemicals in the end.

I dragged the mattress out to the balcony and fell face-first onto it. Insects didn't fall in great numbers. I woke up feeling strange. Was it was dusk or dawn? I went to the bathroom and looked in the mirror. An ugly face looked back. When I was with Colette my face had looked beautiful. How could it be? How could a face be ugly, become beautiful, then turn ugly again?

If I'd been in Milwaukee I would've gone over to her house and begged her to make my face beautiful again. I would've attacked her door, and rubbed mud into my face if she'd said no. In New Orleans, I took my notebook out and wrote.

"Dear Colette..."

But she'd said, "Do not write. Do not call. Do...not...do...anything. Do you hear me?"

That's when I should have slapped her. But I'd never slapped a person in my life. I should have slapped her hard across the face with my right hand and left a red mark on her beautiful cheek. Something for her to think about after I was gone.

We once made molds of our faces using gauze, warm water and Vaseline. It was her idea. She touched my face. It was her idea. We made love on the living room floor. It was her idea. The night before Christmas. Then she flew to Toronto to see her family. Three days later a package came in the mail that smelled of Nag Champa. She'd written a poem.

> I mixed some chocolate in your clay
> while you were away unhappy,
> I was hoping to make your serious work
> play

Five days later I picked her up at the airport in my taxi.

"I'm engaged," she said. "I got engaged to my old boyfriend. The wedding is going to be in June."

"Old boyfriend?"

I wasn't upset. I was like an animal that'd been shot and knew it was dying. I got so drunk I passed out in somebody's backyard in the snow and could have frozen to death. I called her at four in the morning. She didn't answer. I went over to her house. I banged on the door. She said, "We can still be friends, if you really want to be." I cried while she made tea. I came up from behind to hug her. She wheeled and pushed me back. "I'm *engaged*, you can't do that!"

I should have slapped her then too.

It was dusk, not dawn. I knew because the air was cooler. I needed a drink. I carried my bike downstairs over my shoulder. I held my breath in front of the caretaker lady's ugly door. No one lived in the building but her and me. I rode down to the Big Muddy for the first time.

Very industrial. Big heavy machines rusting in tall weeds. Boys playing on a make-shift raft in the water, eight or ten of them, pushing, shoving and shouting.

"Hey, don't tip it over!"

"It's sinking! It's sinking!"

"I'm the captain here!"

"No, I'm the captain, and this is a mutiny!"

The captain pulled out a sword from his belt and stabbed the mutineer.

"Man overboard!"

"Mayday! Mayday!"

"This isn't your ship!"

The captain stabbed another mutineer in the ribs, and the mutineer stabbed the captain in the ribs, and they both fell backwards into the warm river, splash.

Two boys climbed out of the water.

"Shut up, Captain!"

"You talk to me with manner!"

A boy walking the plank wheeled and stabbed the captain through the heart.

They were making it up on the spot. Dying and being reborn in swirling swishing patterns.

I rode away feeling sad.

I found a paved and winding river foot path. An old black man up ahead was sitting on top of the levee by himself on a rock. I climbed up. He was fishing. I stood beside him.

"What are you fishing for?"

No answer.

"Are you fishing for your supper or for recreation?"

There was a five-gallon bucket beside him.

"Ain't caught nothin," he said.

I picked up a rock and skimmed it into the river.

"Don't do that," he said.

"Why not? The fish don't like it?"

"The fish like a calm water. Nothin to disturb it."

I climbed back down to the path. A young white couple were holding hands. They'd just eaten dinner at a fancy restaurant after working all day, all week, all month, for ten years in the same office tower. I whizzed past them without saying "Left!" and the man had to skip a beat to get out of the way.

I heard a car door slam, so I looked. A young man was walking away from the car. "How you doin, dude?" He was alone, talking on a cell phone.

More people were coming down to the river from the parking lot. Nature time. Time to walk the asphalt path that runs along the polluted river at sunset.

Beyond the strip of grass sat huge industrial machines half-buried in tall weeds. The river was brown, stagnant, and stank. But the office workers' love of the black path, surrounded by

a strip of green space on either side, was unpar-
alleled.

I hated them and their day jobs in chicken
cages whose doors swung open at five o'clock,
at which time the workers had license to mill
around the mouth of the cages, asserting
their freedoms by going to a movie or eating
in a restaurant, and on weekends the cage
doors stayed open for two whole days, but on
Monday morning the chickens were expected back inside. They were never supposed to
wander far, so they never did.

A horn honked, so I looked. A young man,
shirt untucked, tie unknotted, was walking
away from the car. I yelled at him, "Stop
honking!" He was talking on his cell phone
loudly, the way people talk on cell phones.
When he merged into the river walk with
the other people I could still hear him. Then
he paced back and forth on the grass, making
hand gestures. But if he and I were standing
side by side, waiting at a crosswalk for the light
to change? I would've taught him a lesson.

A red "Don't Walk" hand is flashing. A car is
driving by. I take a step off the curb into the
crosswalk as if the light had changed, and the
cell phone talking man, oblivious, follows and

is struck by the car. His cell phone flies twenty feet in the air. I step back onto the curb, look around and whistle.

He's down, broken on the street. He looks up at me through dying eyes, blood trickling from his ears, blood burbling from his mouth. I leave him to retrieve the cell phone, then shout into it, "Your friend just died because he was talking to you!" and I hang up.

But he isn't dead. He's only disabled for life. He lives in a convalescent home. He's just twenty-seven years old, and his wife, who was talking to him on the phone at the time of the incident, is traumatized for life, and she cracks up and stops visiting him.

The driver of the car becomes a volunteer at the home. He wants to make it up to the wheelchair-bound man. He wants to ease the man's existential suffering which he believes he caused.

The quadriplegic's wife announces that she loves her husband and is ready to take her place beside him again. Until death do them part. She's a mess. The reasons for her return are murky at best. She's only twenty-three years old. She can't stand living alone. She can't remain celibate for the rest of her life. Life is absurd for the first time.

The driver of the car begins to drink. He loses his job as a middle manager at a tin can factory. When he visits the convalescent home he strikes up a friendship with the wife of the crippled man. They develop a "closeness," followed by a "bond" followed by an intense "physical passion." Their bodies, after sex, fall asleep like ripe cantaloupes that have been left out in the rain.

I wake them up. I say, "You're not the cantaloupe, I'm the cantaloupe!" He asks me to explain. I say, "I don't have to!" and I climb into bed with her. She slaps me in the face. He throws a bottle of champagne at my head and I black out.

Meanwhile, the quadriplegic's mind floats. He has a hard time bringing it back down because he doesn't have a body to bring it back down to. He asks for ever higher doses of various mood stabilizing drugs. He's able to hike high mountain trails for hours on end. He travels across India on the slowest train imaginable. He makes gorgeous love to a certain teenage nursing assistant. He flies through the air. He talks to an eagle. He laughs with the clouds. He floats. He smells the salt breeze of the ocean. He sees the curvature of the earth. He dies in his sleep.

I lay on my back in the tall grass near the river with my arms crossed. It felt nice to kill someone. Murder can be quite a refreshing activity. I took a deep breath. The air smelled pleasant and rotten. Plants were dying at the same time they were being born. I pulled myself off the ground.

It was time to visit the French Quarter. No harm in going where tourists go, as long as I knew I wasn't one of them. I could do the expected sometimes, as long as it wasn't expected of me. I hopped on my bike and ambled.

I made a few wrong turns because I didn't have a map. I didn't understand the crescent thing at all. I came to Bourbon Street. Narrow and quiet. I rode it slowly. Early Tuesday evening. A slim woman realtor carrying a legal-sized yellow notepad walked by with purpose.

I turned off famous Bourbon Street and rode down to the water. I couldn't find it. Tourists were climbing up a tall set of stairs. I climbed up after them. The water was up there. I looked at tall ships with the tourists.

I walked down the stairs and rode along the docks. A different slim woman realtor carrying a legal-sized yellow notepad walked by with purpose. A little jazz band was playing on the street. Talented white kids. A tourist crossing the street turned his hands to snap a picture at waist-level. When he got to the curb he stopped, looked at the picture, and seemed proud of what he'd caught but not seen.

I rode into the next neighborhood. Like the French Quarter but with fewer tourists. I went into a coffeehouse because it had a banana tree in front. The woman behind the counter had large breasts and a thick brown beard. I sat outside with two male hipsters whose heads were buried in laptops.

Three husky black men in white helmets and yellow reflective vests walked into Big Daddy's bar kitty-corner across the street. They came back out. Was Big Daddy's closed? The banana tree coffeehouse was buzzing with jazz from the 40s. The three husky black men looked at us three young white men, then hustled off. Five minutes later they came back.

"Food's good," said one of the hipsters who looked up from his laptop. The other hipster chuckled. I sympathized with what I thought the three black men in white helmets and yellow reflective vests were experiencing.

A minute later, the three black men came out of the coffeehouse. "Wrong place," said one, and they hustled off.

I finished my hot coffee and rode in the direction the three black men had gone. I angled up, away from the river, and turned right. I rode quite a ways, came to a rusty bridge, and rode over it. A long wide channel of water below. I rode into an all-black neighborhood. No whites in sight. I went into a tiny shack or diner.

People were chewing food. The plastic tablecloth was clean and wet from having had a rag recently run over it. I ate a greasy fried egg sandwich with fried onions and questionable mayonnaise. A man at the counter had no teeth. His jaw waggled when he chewed. I would have killed myself. When he talked to the waitress he covered his mouth. The waitress saw me watching, and thought I needed something.

"Are you still working on that?"

"No, I'm not still *working* on that, I'm *enjoying* that!"

She made a face, put one fist on her hip, and walked away.

I gave her a fifty percent tip for being a pain in the ass and rode north, past the poorest, tiniest shacks I'd ever seen. On the left was some kind of raised area of grass that angled up steeply to a tall cement wall. I wanted to cross back over to the French Quarter, but was blocked. I had to turn back.

I hated turning back.

I'd never heard of Café Du Monde, but it was famous. I knew because the napkin said so. It was a big old building, and it was nice to be around tourists. I felt clean and cooled down. I ordered a Western Omelet and ate it fast. My stomach hurt. I ordered coffee with chicory in it, the way it was drank during the Depression. The menu said so.

I saw a loose *Times-Picayune* and picked it up to look at the Want Ads. But first I read an article about sunflowers and blackbirds. Thirteen million acres of sunflowers were under cultivation in the Dakotas, but blackbirds were eating the crop, so farmers had poisoned the blackbirds. Six million dead, same as the Jews. For what reason? For eating two percent of the crop. And, to add insult to injury, the number one use of sunflower seeds? Backyard bird feeders.

"Helper on Shrimp Boat Wanted."

My heart sped up. I tore the ad out and put it in my back pocket. I gave the waitress a one percent tip. Let the tourists make up the difference. I went to find a pay phone.

The shrimper didn't answer, and I couldn't leave a message because I didn't have a phone for him to call me back at, so I hung up and put the ad back in my back pocket. It rubbed against the note left for Darla and the phone number of my best friend's girlfriend's sister.

I put another quarter in the phone and dialed, then hung up because I'd been told that Libby worked at an Irish pub in the French Quarter. So I went looking for an Irish pub in the French Quarter.

A jolly Dixieland band was playing full tilt. The place was big. It had two entrances, one on Bourbon and one on St. Peter. Just a couple of people were in there. I ordered a Pabst Blue Ribbon at the bar. A waitress—great body, long red hair, cute freckled face, amazing beauty— was waiting on a middle-aged Midwestern family. I kept my eye on her golden athletic legs. The father and his teenage son were smitten too.

"Big tips," I muttered.

It had to be Libby. Her sister had red tints in her blond hair, and they both had green eyes and slightly curved noses. Libby was more beautiful though. Too beautiful, in fact. I had her number in my back pocket, a built-in introduction. It could happen in a flash. Things could change. I could be married as fast as Colette was going to be married. Libby's friends could become my friends. I could live in New Orleans.

I ordered a second beer and admired Libby some more. She had to have a boyfriend. Anybody that beautiful had to be taken. Something would be wrong with her if she wasn't already taken. Besides, I'd just killed somebody. Who could love a murderer? Libby could, if she was as beautiful inside as she was outside.

I went to the bathroom. I didn't feel so good. Two greasy egg dinners, and coffee with chicory, and two beers had given me diarrhea. Two men were standing at urinals right next to each other, the urinal to their right unoccupied. How stupid were they? I went into a stall, shut the door and locked it. I tried to be quiet, but couldn't. I waited.

One of the pissers said, "I'm broken."

The other pisser said, "Is that what Beth said?"

The first pisser said, "No, that's what the urinal says."

They both laughed.

After they left I was as loud as I had to be. I flushed and went to investigate. The far right urinal had a sign taped to it that said "I'm broken."

Beth was obviously the pissing man's new girlfriend, and they were always arguing and breaking up and getting back together. She even had him taking Viagra so he could keep up. But he lived with his x-girlfriend, who had a new boyfriend, but they all lived together, and his life without boundaries drove Beth crazy. That was why the pissing man's friend thought Beth had finally said, "I'm broken."

I washed my hands, and as I dropped the paper towel into the waste basket I looked down. An envelope ripped into pieces. I snatched them up. They were damp. I put them in my back pocket with the others, and went back to watch Libby wait on tables.

We met at the bar where she was picking up drinks.

"Hi."

Her face was fresh and open, much more than Colette's. What an easy face to fall into.

"Hi," she said, as she picked up her tray that was loaded down with colored drinks, and carried it off.

"Bye," she said over her shoulder, tossing her long red hair back.

Happy, I biked into a warehouse district next to downtown. Casual-looking twenty-some-things were standing outside a bar called The Economy. They seemed to be artistic, so I hitched my bike to a post and elbowed my way in.

A long narrow space, black walls, not a single window, fucking hot. Opportunity. Bodies pressed together, thick cigarette haze, stink of spilled beer. People scruffily dressed, ragged jeans, worn t-shirts. My kind of people. Men with worried hair, long enough so they could pass their fingers through it when they felt tense. I pushed my way to the bar with twenty other people, edging closer inch by inch. I finally got a beer and made for the sliver of light at the back. A tiny fenced-in area, crowded and loud.

"What's going on!" I shouted to a woman standing next to me.

"Closing!"

"What?"

"For the summer! No air-conditioning!"

A man handed her a beer, and stood beside her.

"My husband!"

They talked like I wasn't there.

He went to the bathroom.

She said to me, "Do you come here a lot?"

"No!"

"We're from Chicago! Down for the weekend! Jazz Fest! Sailing! We like to sail!"

"Of course!"

Her husband came back and she didn't want to talk to me.

It hit me that I didn't know anybody in The Economy bar, or in all of New Orleans—just the caretaker lady, the Siberian guy at the youth hostel, and the guy who'd sold me my bike.

I went and stood by the pool table. A woman was lining up a shot. I watched five men watching her. She was cute as she slid the stick back and forth between her chalked fingers, and the tops of her breasts showed when she leaned in.

"Nice tips," I muttered.

I saw the guy who'd sold me my bike. He was standing by himself, holding a beer in his left hand, his left leg jiggling. Long golden locks flowed down his back, but he was short and shaped like a square, and his shirt was falling off it was so big, and he was snout-faced.

I rode past a thrift store that was open late. I loved New Orleans. I took out my list—it was damp—and went in. I rummaged around. I found a beige drape that I could nail over the stuck window, and a good enough floor lamp for the balcony, and a boxful of *Penthouses* and *Playboys* from the 70s and 80s that I couldn't resist for five bucks.

I rode home with the cardboard box of smut sliding up and down my sweaty right thigh, the heavy drape slung over my left shoulder, the lamp tucked under my sweaty left armpit, the shade resting crookedly on the handle bars.

I missed Magazine Street somehow and wound up on St. Charles. I rode along the gravel next to a railroad tracks for a couple of blocks, then crossed back over, took a bad angle, and my front tire got caught in one of the tracks and I fell, hard. The cardboard box full of smut blocked my heart from being speared on the turned handle bar.

I closed the door behind me. Home sweet home. Then I had sex with about a hundred naked women. That was no way to treat women. But that was no way to treat me.

I showered in the green slimy water that came up to my ankles. I stepped out, remembered I didn't own a towel. I dried myself on my spare shirt. I went to stand on the balcony. The dead dog was still on the curb. I did fifty jumping jacks and looked over the plywood partition for signs of life. I went back inside.

Penthouses and *Playboys* were spread on the couch and floor. I wasn't free. My cock was getting hard again. It was automatic. I was like a dog. I'd been like a dog all my life, or since I was ten.

I started to rip up the pages. But one woman was too beautiful. I carried her into the bathroom, and poked her over a nail that was sticking out. Then I saw more nails, so I went back for more women. When I ran out of nails I pushed women behind bare wires. I squirted dabs of toothpaste on the wall and stuck women on the dabs. I got creative. I cut one woman's breasts off and put them on another woman's chest. I put one woman's head on another woman's shoulders. I put a blond pussy over a brunette pussy. So when I pissed, and brushed my teeth, and washed my hands, and showered, and when I took a shit and shaved, I'd be surrounded by paper naked women, and their power to make me hard would wear off with time and I'd be free.

I put my clothes on and went downstairs to ask the caretaker lady if she had a hammer and nails. She answered the door—did she ever sleep?—and gave me what I wanted. I liked her. I went back upstairs and pounded softly because it was late. Three walls and the inside of the bathroom door were covered. I went out to the balcony. A woman's voice said, "Pussy."

I listened intently.

"Pussy, where are you?"

I leaned over, looked down, saw the top of a woman's head—black hair—searching in the bushes. She was wearing a baggy black sweatshirt like it was November in Wisconsin. A cat meowed, and she lifted it up and carried it inside. I heard a door shut. She lived under me, in the apartment on the other side of the front door.

I pulled the mattress back inside, where I'd put it in the afternoon, and pushed it to the door between the rooms. I shut the door all but a crack. I lay on my stomach and belched. I needed a Tums, or Rolaids, or whatever. I had to sleep on my side so I wouldn't vomit. But I had to sleep on my stomach to sleep.

A woman said I was hogging the bed, so I moved over to the edge of the mattress to give her more room. In the morning I woke up and she wasn't there, and I moved back to the center.

Here Comes the Neighborhood

I biked up to PJ's at two o'clock in the afternoon in the hottest heat. I snuck into the shade of the backyard without ordering anything. I wrote a letter to Colette. I let it flow, stream-of-*conscience* style. I told her that I wished her good luck on her marriage. I told her that I'd found a job "on a fishing boat right outside of Delacroix." I told her that I wanted to kill her, or myself. Signed it, "Tangled up in Blue." I left off my return address because I didn't want her to send it back unopened.

I biked all the way downtown to the main post office. It was cool inside. The marble floor echoed. I stood in a long line, but I didn't mind. Then I retreated, dropped the letter in a big trash can by the entrance—for a hopeful stranger to find.

The sun shone, then it got cloudy, humid and still. I went to the main library to look for information about people from New Orleans. Later I stood next to my bike outside the little Baptist church in the little neighborhood called Black Pearl, where Mahalia Jackson sang as a little girl. It started to pour. I liked getting soaked, but it rained so hard I got cold. I rode until I found an awning in front of a business. The wind was so strong the water in the street made waves. The rain came down in sheets. Cars slowed down, had to stop. Engines stalled out. Cars turned around in search of unflooded routes. Everyone was in a hurry but me.

The sun came out and I walked my bike in ankle-deep warm water, like a pleased flea across the beach of the universe. But being free is one thing, and being without any obligations is another. Nothing ahead, nothing behind. A heavy weight from nowhere bore down on me. I was an unemployed person on vacation. Not a good thing. Whole graveyards of working men were turning over.

Maybe a fiction reading would be a good thing to go to. Maybe I could get shocked. Wasn't that the point of literature? To shock and inspire? But first I had to eat. I found a place on the street that sold Po-Boys. I didn't know what they were. I got a roast beef and gravy. Filled me up good.

Empty folding chairs arranged around an empty podium. White women drinking white wine and chatting. Only two men. I read the poster.

"The best author you have never heard of. James Wilcox's novels are comic masterpieces. In a perfect world his novels would be read by millions and he would have the status of a Phillip Roth or a John Updike."

I'd be the judge of who'd be the judge of that.

I went into the children's play area. A boy toddler had a chair lifted over his head and a girl toddler was sitting with her legs straight out on the blue-and-pink-striped carpet right underneath the chair. The boy dropped the chair. The girl looked at the chair after it landed an inch away from her. The boy pushed the chair in a circle around the room. He stopped. The girl moved her arms up and down like she was a duck. The boy looked at the chair. I went back into the adult room.

"I don't read much fiction anymore, but this book is amazing."

"I'm a voracious reader, but I rarely reread books. Still, I've re-read this novel over and over."

"*Heavenly Days* is the first novel of his I've read, now I want to read them all."

"I was here looking for books on opera, but now I'm ready to read the whole Wilcox oeuvre!"

"If I could I'd move to Tula Springs, maybe take one of those apartments above the Sonny Boy department store."

"He deserves a wider audience."

"He deserves to become more than 'sort of rich.'"

"Quick everyone, tell Oprah!"

A woman asked me if I'd ever read James Wilcox. I confessed I hadn't.

"My advice to you," she said, "is to read the first ten pages, and if you find yourself laughing like a crazy person, then you know this is the book for you. If that doesn't happen, well, I'm sure you've got good taste in some other area of your life."

The chairs were full. I had to squeeze into an empty seat in the center.

"Excuse me, excuse me, excuse me."

The setting was small town southern. The characters were endearing, interlocking incidents ran amok, and the audience tittered. Dialogue sparkled with southern charm. The author loved his well-meaning but bumbling eccentrics who, no doubt, spoke to him in bed and told him what to write about them in the morning. Uproarious chuckling. A baby behind me let out a horrified scream.

I turned around to see who the intelligent child was.

A man hissed, "Haven't you ever heard a baby scream before?"

I hissed back, "Haven't you ever seen somebody turn around to look at a baby scream before?"

"No!"

"Then you must be amazed by the uniqueness of the situation that we find ourselves in!

"Excuse me, excuse me, excuse me."

I had to put some fresh air between myself and those Tula Springs people. I'd put myself in a ridiculous situation, and then I'd had an upsetting altercation. Life was wonderful.

The next morning I put on my damp shirt and thought about Libby, and how she was possible. And I thought about the cat woman downstairs, and how she was possible. Then I thought about coffee and remembered the pieces of envelope in my back pocket that I'd found in the waste basket.

I pulled them out. They were still damp. I put them together. It was easy, a letter ripped three times, a total of eight pieces.

Hi = Lois its John. Got your letter and I
was very impressed and happy,. Lois this
is how I would love to Start, I want to
eat, lick, & suck your Asshole & Cunt.
French kiss you, Fuck you with a vibrator
and Strap on Dildo. 69 and that goes with
it Would love it, if you gave me a Hot
Blowjob!! Let me know when we can meet
on Layovers! This is how I would like to
start, Would love for you to come layover
with me Everymonth please! Let me know
your workload schedule.

Lois heres the $25.00 Dollars for the
photos. Heres my phone Number. John.
504-933-7379. Lustfully Yours. Lois
watersports masturbation Blowjobs 69
Dildo Fucking. John H III. P.S. Lets Be
Close & Intimate Friends & Lovers Shall
We Lois Statement: Me or I John H.
Cleveland III am Not out to Entrap you
and I am not a LAW enforcement officer,
Yours,

John H. Cleveland III.

John of little substance, handwriting huge
and childish. The letter had been returned
unopened, marked "Return to Sender," then
tossed in the trash. Ridiculous John, what had
he expected? Was he so stupid to think Lois
would take him up on his potty-mouthed sex
gambit? Then again, Lois had written to him,

and John had been impressed, and been made happy by what she had written. Could she be as crazy as John? Had she really sent nude photographs? Had John been in the bar when I picked up the pieces? Would he have been obvious to recognize? Can you tell a crazy person just by looking at them?

I sat on the tin floor of the balcony and felt glad I wasn't tangled up with anyone. I was free. But Libby was possible, and the woman below was possible, and I was beginning to fill up with that strange jelly-like substance again.

"Eric, you over there?" a voice said.

I didn't have time to run and hide, and a face popped around the Greek column and looked at me. It was an adolescent boy's face, seventeen or eighteen years old.

"Where's Eric?"

"I live here now."

"You sell pot?"

"No."

"Eric sold pot. God, I don't want to go back out on the street."

The face withdrew.

I had a neighbor.

I could hear him moving and scratching around on the other side of the partition like a mouse.

I said, "Is Eric black?"

He popped his face back around the column.

"Yeah, why?"

"No reason."

He looked at me like I should say more.

"My name's Nick," I said.

"Hey, my name's Nick too!"

He shook my hand hard, like having the same name meant something. Like our parents had been thinking the same mystical thoughts when we were conceived, or at least reading the same baby name books.

He ducked back around the column and disappeared. I scratched my chin that I hadn't shaved in over a week.

To get over this, I biked Uptown to PJ's. A young woman, chewing gum and drinking coffee, sat by the front window. She had a tattoo on her left bicep of barbed wire with a heart inside it, as common as pony tails and jump ropes once were.

She had one leg resting on the chair in front of her, a square white bandage on its tan shin. She looked up as I came in, then back down. She chewed long after the sugar was gone, I was sure of that.

"Small coffee to go," I said.

I rubbed my hands together. They felt soft. No need for hand lotion here. I decided to get a haircut.

I was afraid to go to a black barber, but I wanted to go to a black barber. There wasn't a sign that said I couldn't go in, but there was a force field.

I pushed myself in the back. I sat down. Five men stopped talking and looked at me. I didn't look at them. They started talking again. I looked at magazines. *Swank, Juggs, Hustler, Players, Knave, Screw. Players* had a black woman on the cover. The images were way too raunchy for me.

Nobody paid attention to me. Was I in line? How long would I have to wait? I waited. I flipped through the magazines a second time. I got waved over to a swivel chair.

The barber was large and smelled good, and he was friendly. But he didn't talk. I wasn't sure if he wasn't curious, or if he was rude, or if he was tired, or if he saw so many hundreds of people every week that he just didn't feel like talking. I didn't talk either. I just hoped he'd cut my hair right.

He held a mirror up so I could see the sides and back. It was too short! I didn't ask for that! Why had he done that to me? My hair wasn't long enough to worry now! I wanted to rip into him, but I tipped him five bucks instead.

Out on the street again, a Harley-Davidson —"the pride of Milwaukee"—blatted past. Then a whole gang of them came, one by one. It took a full minute for them to get past, while I was forced to suspend my thoughts and wait.

For a long time I could hear them in the distance downshifting, upshifting, and down-shifting. Finally, it was quiet and I shouted, "Long-haired assholes, think it's so great to make a neighborhood stop thinking while you roll by!"

My stomach growled. It wanted meat.

I hesitated.

"There's a McDonald's!" said my stomach. "Should we go in?"

"You're embarrassing me!" said my stomach.

"Don't do it. The meat's from a cow nobody loved, and while it was employed it wasn't paid for its labor, not a penny."

"You think too much," said my stomach.

We went into McDonald's.

I ordered off the Dollar Menu. Double cheeseburger, McChicken sandwich, small fries, small drink, chocolate sundae. I went outside carrying three bags.

Down the block, a construction crew lay slumped, dead-looking under a large shade tree. Had they all been shot? Some of their lunch pails were open, others were closed. They were all taking naps, sent off to soft sleep by singing birds and traffic.

I ate standing up. Then I pedaled slowly home.

I stood on the balcony and looked across the street. I hadn't noticed the large apartment building over there. Ugly 70s edifice.

A Mexican, Guatemalan, or Salvadorian man came outside and crouched on the ground in the sun. He fiddled with a stick in the dirt.

He was used to living in a house like a barn where he was one of the animals. Now he lived in an apartment with hallways and no balconies, and the only way he could be outside on his one day off a week was to take his keys, walk down the hall, go down the stairs, open the fire door, crouch on the bare ground next to the sidewalk, and run a bit of filthy dirt through his fingers.

A black man came out of the building and the Mexican stood up. The Mexican was much shorter. The black man talked and the Mexican didn't smile. Then a little black boy, about four years old, came out of the building in a flash and ran down the sidewalk. I went back inside to lay down.

Whatever of Darla's that had once been wet on the mattress was dry now. I thought of the drug-dealer man named Eric. A bullet for Darla would be a bullet for me. I hoped he had good aim. Nobody wants to be a quadriplegic.

I once took a nap while Colette read in a chair. She woke me up and suggested we go for a walk in the falling snow. I agreed that a walk would be nice. "Wake me up," I said, and fell back asleep. An hour later she woke me up and said, "Do you want to study Spanish?" I said "I don't know, do you feel like it?" She shrugged and walked into the kitchen. Thirty minutes later we put our coats on and went outside. She walked past her car and I said, "I thought we were going to study Spanish." She said, "I thought we were going for a walk."

We were like that.

I was sitting on the tin floor in my cut-offs with my back to the brick wall because I didn't feel safe being naked anymore, when I heard a knock on the plywood partition.

"Come in," I said sarcastically.

The boy's face popped around the column.

"What's up?"

"You want to come have a beer with us?"

"Us?"

"Me and my girlfriend."

"I don't know, maybe next time."

He held the column in both hands and shimmied around. He landed softly on my side. He was slight of build, maybe five foot six, and wasn't wearing a shirt. He had a wisp of damp chest hair in the center, just a wisp. The hair on his head was blond and tousled, like it might be worried one day when he got older. His belly was flat, like an untroubled boy's belly. He was the boy next door. The kind of boy who smokes pot every day and doesn't have a paranoid bone in his body.

"How old are you?" I said.

"Nineteen. How old are you?"

"Thirty."

"You're eleven years older than me."

He was good at math.

"Where you from?"

"Milwaukee. Where you from?"

"Detroit."

One hell of a conversation.

"I came down for Mardi Gras and never left—and you?"

I didn't want to tell him, and besides he probably wouldn't remember what I said, so I didn't say anything.

"Hey, I gotta piss—mind if I?" And he skimmed past me, into the apartment and toward the bathroom where women were cut up into parts and nailed to the walls and stuck behind exposed wires and jammed into cracks and pushed into gobs of toothpaste.

I thought of jumping off the balcony and breaking my neck. I thought of running down the stairs, leaping three at a time, and disappearing for a couple of years.

He came back.

"Pornography's not really my thing. But more power to you."

"Pornography's not really my thing either."

He was listening.

"It's an...exhibit. A pinup...installation. You've heard of the word 'pinup,' haven't you?"

"Sure."

"Well...you know how society divides women up into parts, right? So I was mirroring that. 'Women as Pinup.' That'll be the name of the installation if I ever do it. On a larger scale, of course."

He shrugged.

"Ah shit," I said, "I found a box of magazines at that thrift store on Jefferson, and..."

"I love that place! They got great stuff!"

"I know, so for five bucks I..."

"You ever go to that thrift store on Carondelet? It's even better!"

"I'll have to get over there. Hey, you want to see some other pictures?"

"Pictures?"

He looked at me like I really was a pornographer.

"I found them in the apartment."

When I came back with the pictures of the three black men he was sprawled on the couch like he lived there. Calm bastard.

"That one's Eric," he said, pointing.

It was the tall guy standing in the kitchen about to ladle hot food into his mouth after he'd blown on it for a few seconds.

"Did Eric live with anyone?"

"His girlfriend."

"Darla?"

"I think that was her name."

"Was she black?"

"No, white. Why?"

I didn't say anything. I'd have to imagine the whole scenario over again.

"I sure wish you sold dope, man. I hate to go back out on the street."

He looked around at the kitchen table, the chairs, the bare walls, the mattress on the floor. He walked around. He examined the blue ladder with his hands. I knew what he was doing. He was thinking! He was thinking of what he was going to tell his girlfriend about the crazy guy upstairs who had porn on his bathroom walls!

"I never been in here before," he said.

"You always dealt across the partition?"

"Yeah."

He walked out to the balcony, grabbed the column with both hands and swung himself around.

"See you later."

Not ten minutes later a face appeared at an angle around the column, long black hair falling straight down.

"I'm Julie."

It was the woman I'd seen looking for the cat in the bush.

"Hi, I'm Nick."

"Two Nicks, ha. That's funny. I must have a dull razor!"

She slapped her bare knee and opened her mouth and shut her eyes like she was laughing. Then she wrapped both arms around the column and tried to shimmy around, but got stuck half way, and I had to help. I didn't mind. I touched her wrist, it was fine. Fine nose, high cheekbones, pale complexion. Not the kind of face you want to reduce to points of interest.

I glanced at her breasts, but couldn't tell what shape they were because they were hidden under the same black sweatshirt she'd worn the night before.

"Nick told me about your 'Bathroom Installation.' He tells me everything—mind?" And before I knew it, she'd skimmed past me. I didn't even bother to want to jump off the balcony or run down the stairs. She came back in less than a minute.

"Reminds me of a story. Are you coming to Finn McCool's with us?"

"Finn McCool's?"

"A hole-in-the-wall, very unhip."

"I don't know, I'm pretty tired."

"Do you work?"

"No."

"Me neither. What kind of work do you do when you work?"

"Cab driver."

"Are you an artist?"

"No."

"Nobody in New Orleans has a real job. Nick's a poet, did he tell you?" She recited a poem in William Burroughs' tired, dry voice.

Friday night is a soft corner workers land in
Saturday is kinder for what follows
Sunday sighs
"Pick up your x and grind"

I laughed.

"Nick wrote 'pick up your *axe* and grind,' but I made him change it to *x*. It sounds more existential that way, don't you think?"

"Sure."

"So you're coming? I'll tell you the story if you do."

"Okay."

Finn McCool's

I thought Finn McCool's would be close by, but it took twenty minutes to drive there in Julie's black Saab. I didn't know what route we took, or what neighborhood it was even in. I was just along for the ride.

A cool dive. Wooden booths, laid back, mostly empty. I watched Nick standing at the bar trying to flag down the lazy bartender while Julie hand-rolled a cigarette with her long fingers.

Nick came back balancing three pints, and Julie put a cigarette between her lips. She had chocolate-brown eyes. I liked chocolate. I thought of her black hair mingling with Libby's red hair, falling on my legs, as both of them kissed me and loved my cock. Colette had dishwater hair.

Julie began to tell the story.

"I moved to Toronto when I was twenty-one, into a ghetto neighborhood by the freeway with some friends from college. A hermit lived next door in an old clapboard house—I don't even really know what clapboard means. Let's just say the house needed 'massive repairs.' Every window was boarded up. Or cardboarded up, actually."

Toronto. Colette's hometown. I hated Toronto.

Julie continued.

"The front steps were covered with junk. Trees were actually growing on the roof of his house. Can you imagine that? He was like a wild nocturnal animal. We saw him standing on the back steps sometimes at night, staring off at nothing.

"We lived in a once-grand Victorian flat with high lofted ceilings. An excellent place for young would-be artists to waste a year or three before going to graduate school. Anyway, he was like a feral cat nobody could touch. He had a mind and rhythm of his own. He'd once lived in the house with his wife, and when she died he let things go. We just assumed that. People assume all kinds of things all the time. It's natural, don't you think? Can you feel the tension building?"

She took a swig of beer.

"One day an ambulance came and they carried him out on a stretcher, his face covered.

The house stood empty for a week, then a month, then for a couple of months. Then one night, when we were high on Ecstasy and rum, we decided to go over there. What a combination, huh? We were playing 'ethnoarcheologist' and I was the leader because I had a flashlight! We were breaking and entering, and that's a capital crime. Our hairs stood on end, not literally, but we were middle class kids, you know, and we were going to break into a dead man's house."

She asked Nick to get her another beer, although hers was half full. She rolled another cigarette, and I looked at her face. My stomach hurt—from the story, or because I hadn't eaten anything? Finn McCool's only had potato chips and pickles. Nick came back. He tapped his feet nervously on the wooden floor, and spit between his legs.

Julie looked at him and said, "That's disgusting." Then she took a drag on her cigarette and went on.

"This is where the story really begins. The hermit had created a, get this, museum of debauchery. Every square inch of wall space in his house, on the first floor at least—we were too freaked out to go upstairs—was covered with, and I mean *covered with*, pornographic images."

She let that sink in.

"Entire walls were devoted to various body parts. He had a breast wall, a vagina wall, a belly wall, a lip wall, an eye wall." She ticked them off on her fingers. "He had a hairy bush wall, a black hairy bush wall, a blond hairy bush wall, a shaved bush wall." She inhaled as if she were out of breath. "He had every kind of wall you can think of. It was wonderful—if you could get past the gross-out factor—but that's not even the most salacious part."

She let that sink in.

"Let's go outside. It's hot in here, don't you think?"

We went into the backyard. A simple patch of cement with some lawn furniture scattered around. I breathed in the night air. A man sitting on a lawn chair by himself was going to get an earful.

Julie wasn't in a hurry though. She rolled another cigarette, and I saw the man sitting on the lawn chair gaze at her long fingers, and at her long hair and wide mouth. She was wonderful to look at.

Julie looked up and gave me a slanted, knowing smile.

She continued.

"He even had an ankle wall, subdivided into many different types of *ankles*. I'm not an ankle authority, mind you, so I wasn't able to parse the nuances of the ankles, but it must have taken him years to create. I guess that's what happens when you spend your whole life alone."

She leaned in and whispered, "But that's not even the most interesting part."

She puffed her cigarette and the man we didn't know pulled his chair in a little bit closer.

"The shower rod had women's underwear hanging on it. Old, encrusted, grimy underwear that was hard to the touch, and brittle. It came off in flecks. The clothespins were the old-fashioned kind.

"Were they his wife's underwear? Had she died suddenly, and he hadn't had the heart to take them down? Or had he never had a wife? Were the undergarments a fantasy? A way to pretend that he had a wife and a normal life? All I know is we almost puked at the sight of the stuff!"

The man we didn't know said, "I had a landlord once who fucked his dog. I don't know that for a fact, but he seemed to like the dog 'a little too much,' if you know what I mean. And nobody, I mean nobody ever came to visit him."

Julie took a drink and her throat throbbed. I thought how strange it would be to kiss that throat now, knowing that she was a monologist.

"But who am I to judge? We're all freaks. It's just a matter of admitting it, and to what extent. But admitting you're a freak—in this society? Someone said once, 'There are three kinds of self: public, private, and secret.' And I believe that, because if you ever go public with your private self, or dare to even go private with your secret self—then watch out, you're in for a fucking shit storm!"

She threw her half-smoked cigarette into her half-full bottle.

"I don't like lukewarm beer. Beer should come in six ounce bottles. Don't you think?" And she lit a new cigarette. I guessed that she came from a wealthy family.

"So," she said to me, "has my story stopped you from going off the deep end?"

What? Was it my turn to talk? Did I have to come clean? Did I have to explain myself with honesty or something? How could I, when I didn't know?

I cleared my throat. I cleared it again. I had to say something. Or could I just make something up?

"How long do you think he was dead before they found him? I mean, if he was a hermit and all, how would anyone have known he was dead?"

She frowned.

The man we didn't know jumped in. "I think he visited a whore on the first of every month—on the day he cashed his SSI and Disability checks—and when he didn't show up, bam, the whore called the cops."

"Bravo!" said Julie.

I'd flunked, and the stranger had gotten an A.

Julie said, "When in the absence of facts—and this is the constant state of human affairs—you just have to make it up. This is the answer to most of the riddles of human existence, if I may be so bold."

Nick laughed, and said, "I don't think the hermit saw a particular whore on a regular basis, because that would've meant he had a connection to somebody, so technically he wouldn't have been a hermit."

"Bravo!"

She looked at me.

The man we didn't know stood up and said, "Well, it was nice to have met ya'll."

"What are you thinking?"

"Nothing."

"But everyone is always thinking something. What are you thinking?"

"Nothing."

She turned to Nick. "Can you believe the way Rory treated Stacy today?"

"That sure was cool when she slammed him into that mirror. All that blood."

They laughed.

"Who are Rory and Stacy?"

"Soap opera characters. Don't you watch any soaps?"

"I don't have a TV."

Julie looked at Nick. Nick looked at Julie.

"You want to borrow my TV?" said Nick.

"No."

"Why not?"

"I'd watch it."

"Isn't that the point of having a TV?" said Julie.

"I mean I'd watch it all the time. It'd be like ...having heroin in the house."

"'Like having heroin in the house'—may I use that? With your permission, of course."

"Sure."

"You seem nervous."

"No I'm not."

"You look nervous."

I stood up, stretched my arms above my head, then touched my toes. It looked like I might be getting ready to run. I didn't owe her anything.

"I'm worried about you," said Julie.

She was worried about me? She'd only known me an hour, how could she be worried about me? Then it came to me that Nick was the boy who'd help carry the dead dog across the street, so I said, "Nick, did you help carry a dead dog across the street a couple of nights ago?"

"That was me."

Julie pulled her pouch of tobacco out and began to roll.

"Nick, did you really help carry a dog across the street two nights ago, and not tell me?"

"Yeah."

He swung his feet back and forth on the rough cement, and Julie put her tobacco away and went inside Finn McCool's.

I said to Nick, "Was he on a leash?"

"No."

"God damn it!"

"Hey man, it's New Orleans, chill out."

"What do you mean 'chill out'? He was a black dog out at night, not on a leash. It's the owner's fault!"

"Yeah, well, do you know what it's like to live with a leash around your neck?"

"No."

"Well, neither do I. So it died running—what more could a dog want?"

The Outhouse and a Good Marriage

A woman jumped off the balcony. I looked down at the bush, but couldn't see her. "She must be hurt," I thought, and threw on my pants and shirt, and ran barefoot down the stairs. I looked in every corner of that bush, but she wasn't in there. I walked up the stairs and got back into bed before I realized there hadn't been a woman.

I slept ten hours, like a rotten piece of lumber. I never wanted to get out of bed again. They say Hemingway woke up happy every morning, ready to write no matter how black the night before had been. My legs started to ache, so I got up. I tip-toed to the balcony. The tin was pleasing to my toes. I hopped up to see over the partition. Nobody there.

Then I remembered—I had neighbors. I went to piss. I saw the body parts all over the walls. I ripped them off in a fury. I jumped up and down on them. I stuffed them in a plastic bag. I tied the knot tight. I took the bag down to the garbage can in back of the building. I lifted what was in there out, dropped my bag on the bottom, and covered it over with layers.

I walked to the end of the balcony, and looked off to the left. A ramshackle white family was on the lawn in front of a white house, in the shade under a tree. A thin older man, who looked long-term unemployed, stood watching two fat women so obese they had to spread their legs wide to get close to a low table they were playing checkers on.

A gangly fourteen-year old boy came out of the house and the old man picked up a green garden hose that was hiding in the grass and squirted the boy who squealed and dodged out of the way. The boy grabbed the hose out of the old man's hands and chased him, threatening to soak him, but never quite (on purpose) caught up to him. The old man, whose joints were rickety from a life of labor, or from no labor at all, ran and the boy chased and squealed.

The old man managed to get into an old Oldsmobile that was parked at the curb. He locked the doors. The boy squirted the windshield, and the old man ran the windshield wipers. The boy laughed so hard he had to grab his crotch. The old man lit a cigarette and coughed. The car filled up with smoke and the boy fell down on the tar it was so funny. The two fat women playing checkers didn't look up.

I thought the old man might die of lung cancer, trapped in the car. The boy tried the passenger door, and the old man rolled down the window, and threw his cigarette butt out. The boy shouted, "Not fair!" and ran back around to the driver's side squirting. The old man crossed his arms like he could wait fifty years. The boy dropped the hose in disgust, and walked over to the women playing checkers.

The old man snuck out of the car, tip-toed over to the hose. But the boy was only fooling, he wheeled and grabbed the hose and soaked the old man good, right in the face, on his shirt, and all over the front of his pants. The two fat women laughed so hard they about burst their fat seams. The old man, his arms held out like a zombie, walked into the house to find a towel.

Red-haired Libby's phone number was suddenly burning a hole in my back pocket, and I went looking for a pay phone.

Colette once took me sledding. I hadn't been sledding since I was a kid. We picked up two sleds from her house and walked to a park that had a hill. I hadn't even noticed that park had a hill. It was late at night and nobody was there but us. A black, cold sky. We bounced over bumps, crashed into fences, but mostly we landed softly. We kissed in the snow that was falling on cue. We climbed up that hill a hundred times before she got hungry. I was happy to go home with her. We lay on the rug next to the heat register, my head on her lap, her mouth moving upside down while she talked. Everything was wonderful. Nothing could harm us. She lay on her back and put one hand behind her head so her elbow poked up like a tent. I pulled down her pants. Later, she sang Joni Mitchell songs while I cooked pasta. Things were perfect, and would always be.

> Colette Fuck you
> you are a Cunt
> I don't Ever Want to See You agin

But instead of calling Libby, I called the number of the guy who needed help on the fishing boat. No answer. Must have been out fishing. Too bad. I could have used the work. To have work is to be able to come home from work. To work is to dig yourself every day out of the hole that fills in over you again at night. Work is to use your fishing muscles.

I stood at a crosswalk waiting for the light to change. A young mother and her son, about seven years old, sat in a car idling in front of me. She reached over to pat down his messy, pre-worried hair. A second later he mussed it up again to restore himself.

The world of human acts.

The light changed and they drove off. I crossed the street.

I missed someone—not Colette, or Libby—but someone. Someone I'd probably never meet.

I walked over to Curley's Diner, two blocks away, to use the pay phone to call Libby. I'd never been in there because the ceiling was low and false and there were a lot of brown stains in places.

"Two eggs, toast, hash browns...over easy ...whole wheat...just water, please."

I leaned over the counter to grab a left-over newspaper. I bumped the salt shaker. The cover wasn't screwed on tight, and I had to shovel spilled salt into the palm of my hand and dump it into the ashtray. What else could go wrong?

The waitress came back with an unlit cig-arette in one hand and a glass of ice water in the other. She was tall, middle-aged, and thin as a rail. Her face was wrinkled. Her face was brown. So much smoke had swirled into her face over the last thirty years that her face had turned brown. Her face was weathered. She had a weathered face.

In the beginning she'd been a child, but things hadn't gone as planned. There was a bad marriage to a high school sweetheart (a controlling alcoholic), bad overhead lighting, brats for kids, trouble with the law, stolen TVs hidden in the crawl space under the house, truancy until they quit school at fourteen to work as tire repairmen, phone answerers, and cement mixers. The little red rose of the waitress's early face.

She was in the process of gathering up the ketchup bottles and putting them in a row on the counter to refill. What a nice job. I watched her carefully, and she never shot me the evil eye.

Her face was harrowed. She had a harrowed face. She had a plowed face. Her face had been plowed by circumstances beyond her control. Circumstances were etched into her thin, weathered, etched, plowed face.

My food came and I tried to shake ketchup on my hash browns, but the ketchup was stuck, then it spurted out across my plate and on the counter. I tried to wipe it up with a napkin, but the napkin was too small, so I reached over the counter to pull more napkins out of the dispenser, but she'd packed them in too tight, so I had to use my sticky hand to hold the dispenser while I pulled at the clump of napkins with my other hand, which left ketchup smudges on the freshly-cleaned metal dispenser, which I had to wipe off using more napkins that I had pull out.

I looked at the newspaper while I ate. The Sports section was the most important section to me. The Lakers scored 120 points and still lost. The Brewers scored one run and won. The court, the diamond, the grid iron, the course, the track. How easy to live in forms that were built by previous generations for me to live in.

The waitress told me to have a nice day. I told her I'd try. She followed me outside. I looked back. She was leaning against a dumpster, lighting up a cigarette using a lighter. I preferred matches to lighters.

I walked away with my hands in my pockets, the way a lot of men walk if you look at them. I checked in my back pocket for Libby's number. Wrinkled but readable. I heard a bus coming. I ran to catch it. I didn't want to know where it was going. I had hopes for that bus. It dumped me off in The French Quarter.

I sat on a park bench, put my head in my hands and cried. I ran to find a pay phone, but couldn't find one. Then I found one, but it was smashed up. Then I found one, but its guts had been ripped out by the phone company. Why had I smashed my cell phone in an airport men's room?

I thought back.

Oh yeah, Colette.

And I thought back to the boy I'd once been. The actor, the playful kid, the boy who'd been able to fly in his dreams just by standing on a hill and opening his jacket. How angry that kid must be now—to be so deprived!

I stood on the balcony. For a long time I just stood there, touching the railing, leaning against the brick, standing with my arms crossed, leaning into the railing, letting my arms hang. I couldn't think of anything to do.

I went downstairs to get the mail. I stood in front of the caretaker lady's smelly door for ten minutes. I stood in the front doorway looking out at the apartment across the street.

A frail, thin woman about sixty years old was walking slowly from the front door to a lawn chair ten feet away. She dragged one leg, and the arm on that side hung down. She made it to the chair. The four-year-old boy I'd seen running before came scampering out of the building. He hugged the old woman's leg. She bent down and held him, kissed him, and let him go. He ran down the sidewalk. She waved me over. Who, me? She cupped her hand for me to come. So I went.

She told me she'd been shot in the head. I tried to imagine it. She said her boyfriend had broken his leg jumping out a window, "to get away from some people." She said, "That boy is Nate, he's my grandson." Nate came scampering back. He hugged my leg. He wanted me to walk with him hanging on my leg but I said "No, I can't do that." But he wouldn't let go, and the grandma said, "It's okay," so I walked with him hanging on my leg and he laughed and begged me to do it again. Then he ran off down the sidewalk again.

"Kids are a lot of fun," I said.

"I can't hear too well," she said.

I was glad she was friendly and not angry at me for looking like one of the white people who were gentrifying the neighborhood. Then a man came out of the building and yelled at Nate. "Come over here!" and he grabbed the boy by both arms and yanked him. "I don't want you ever doing that!" Then he picked the boy up roughly and carried him inside.

"Yes," said the grandma, "I got shot in the head a long time ago, baby. And my boyfriend got a broken leg jumping out a window to get away from some people. He's in jail now. You know, that don't seem right. They stabbed him in the arm and he jumped out a window. But that's life, I guess. That's my son Tony."

As I was walking back across the street she said, "Twenty-five stitches!" I turned around to look. "And he was just trying to stop his best friend from beating up a girl."

I pedaled all the way Uptown without stopping. I moved my legs in tight small circles. It didn't make me feel better though. The French Quarter, Mardi Gras, Bourbon Street, Streetcar Named Desire, Big Muddy, Jazz, Crescent City, Superdome, Lake Pontchartrain, all those famous names—I wanted to puncture them! I, the pioneer, who hadn't bought a *Lonely Planet* guidebook from Borders, or a laminated foldable *Streetwise* map from The Travel Store! I, who hadn't fed my brain pre-masticated information!

I came to a small library. I decided to go in. A young woman was sitting on the grass outside, leaning up against the brick wall. Her eyes were closed. She wore black socks that came up to her knees. Her hands were tucked under her ass. I went inside, shut my eyes and pulled five books at random off the shelf: *Old Blue Eyes. The Alchemist. The Story of Christianity Volume 2. Dummies Guide to Economics. Oxford German Dictionary.* I took them to a table. The black-socked woman came in and sat at a table near me. She flipped through the pages of a magazine, looking at the pictures. She picked up another magazine and did the same. She was bored, and boring to look at. And the librarian was listless, like he'd never been happy. He worked in the right place then. A man crossed his arms and lifted his elbows above his shoulders, then squeezed to relieve tension.

I went outside. The sun was shining. A book lay on the sidewalk in front of me. I looked to the right, I looked to the left. I waited for someone to pick it up. I inspected. It wasn't a library book, just a cheap paperback. Now it was mine.

"Iced coffee."
"Tall or Grande?"
"Just give me the biggest one."
"Room for milk?"
"Milk is for babies."

"What?"

"Nothing."

"That'll be two dollars and three cents."

"Three cents?"

"Yeah."

"Isn't that kind of ridiculous?"

"What?"

"Three cents."

"I don't set the prices."

"But you agree that it's ridiculous, right?"

"I don't know, it could be."

I took my iced coffee into the backyard. A young woman with popsicle-lime bra straps sat down near me. She was the most beautiful woman there. A young man sat down beside her. He was too young and immature for her. He looked at me. A man looking at a man looking at a woman—he stared me down in less than two seconds in order to protect her from being projected upon.

I picked my notebook up and began to write the preface of *Buy a Bike New Orleans*. I wanted to explain that I'd started out as an imitator like everyone else, but I'd been transformed by a journey in New Orleans. A woman with Colette's small build walked by, balancing a muffin on a stack of text books. I had to get out of there.

I walked through the heat into the air-conditioning, and back out into the heat in front. The U.S. was living on life support. From Phoenix to Los Angeles, and from Milwaukee to Miami, human beings were living where they didn't belong, in large numbers that couldn't be supported without burning massive amounts of fossil fuels for heating and cooling.

People think fossil fuels come from fossils, but the true meaning of "fossil" is anything you dig up from the ground, including oil. I read that.

I zigzagged on my bike south and east, down to the river. Another berm, or wall, interrupted me. Where was the river? I couldn't break through to it. Cement factories, other factories, big trucks. Not such a sweet sight. I took a side street back up, found a vacant lot that ran along a railroad track. Tall grass and weeds. Industrial music coming from a house at the end of the vacant lot. Iron pipes beating, snare drums snapping, some kind of high-pitched whining. I pushed my bike through tall weeds to find the source of the music.

Two freight trains were scraping and squawking past each other on a sidetrack!

I followed one of the trains, then turned around after it disappeared around a corner in the crooked distance.

And still night was a long way off.

I came to Audubon Park. It was huge. An eighteen hole golf course. I rode around it, hating each water-guzzling, golf-cart-driving idiot. I found some shade and crashed my bike into an ancient oak tree. I lay down and covered my eyes with my arm, my elbow sticking up like Colette's tent. I took it down. I thought of Julie and the hermit. I thought of creating a website instead of a book. A website would create more buzz. I'd be able to sell advertising for bikes, shithole apartments, things people didn't normally advertise. I'd create a niche market for cheapfuck weirdoes like myself. I took my notebook out to write down some ideas.

A chapter called "No Maps, Don't Plan."

"The city will unfold before you. Routes will appear before you as you ride. No expectations!"

A chapter called "Go, Don't Know."

"The goal is to not even know what city you're in. Sure, it'll be hard, but would you want it to be easy?"

A chapter called "I Did It, So Can You."

"You'll need a friend to buy your airplane ticket, and take you to the airport, and guide you blindfolded to the departure gate, and explain to the TSA agents, stewardesses, and pilot, etc."

I pushed my notebook away. Writing was hard, and I was lazy. But to put readers in a position to sit on a bike on a residential street and not know what city they were in? That was a noble cause.

But who was I to write a guidebook like no other guidebook? Who was I to incorporate myself as Buy a Bike International, LLC? become its CEO, and sprout hundreds of entrepreneurs underneath me?

Who was I?

My bike was gone, and I panicked. My bike had been stolen. There it was, over there. Twisted on the grass, in front of the oak tree I'd smashed it into.

But if it had been stolen?

I would have cried and looked in all five corners of the world for my white Giant! I would have vowed never to love again! I would have wept face-down in the tall weeds away from prying eyes, because she wasn't just a bike, she was a *cross* bike.

Then I would have replaced her, of course. Because, after all, bikes are all alike.

I thought of contacting the Giant bike company, and asking them to advertise on my website. They would take a picture of me straddling my bike, a wide smile on my face.

A false smile from someone you love can be worse than a kick in the balls—if you have balls, that is—because in that instant the one you love has vacated the face that made you less lonely and more lovely.

Colette, who was so good at smiling.

Another forty-five minutes were dead and gutted, and still the sun wasn't close to being down.

I heard water trickling from a fountain. I sat up, saw a naked boy sitting on the back of a turtle, the turtle spitting a jet of water out of its mouth. And then a man dropped down to his knees and began snapping photographs of a woman standing above him. She twirled for the camera as he circled below. He went down on his back. She was maybe eighteen, he was maybe forty. She was wearing a shiny, short, red leather skirt. She had a small black leather purse slung over a shoulder, the other was bare. Her makeup was thick, or seemed thick because she was outside in the sun and not in a dark nightclub. What were they selling? Skirt, purse, or makeup? There was no way to tell. It reminded me of a Xerox copy of a photograph that I'd had on my wall in Milwaukee— of an old, serious, dedicated painter, hunched over, paunch-bellied, gray straggly hair, shabby clothes, who was painting a beautiful nude woman on a large canvas...and on the other side of the canvas? The young nude herself, half-sitting on a stool, one leg raised, the foot resting on a rung, the other foot, heel raised off the floor, both legs turned in slightly for added coyness, an insinuation of shadow between the legs, a hint of riches, a vortex to fall into.

I had a dream once—what, a whole three months ago?—that I was in love with a woman —not Colette—and we were about to be married. But I had a secret hiding place that I'd never told anyone about—a place where I went to lick my wounds whenever things went off the rails—and I wanted to tell her about it, otherwise the marriage would be a sham. But when I tried to tell her, I couldn't do it. Then, the night before the wedding, we had a huge fight and I ran away—to the sunny side of the outhouse, where I sat warming my face with my eyes closed, and I thought, "I can't get married!" and I went back to tell her the wedding was off, but the words that came out were, "I want to tell you about my secret hiding place!" And the next day we were married. Total bliss! True marriage!...Later, after we'd had our first disagreement, I ran away to the sunny side of the old outhouse to hide and warm my face. She came to me said, "I've come to be with you." I said, "No, you've come to *get* me!" She said, "No, I've come to *be* with you. There's a difference. And besides, you told me where to find you."

I was afraid to tell Colette that dream. I was afraid because we were going to tell each other everything!

Intellectual Drifter

I was under a building with a black woman.
We were down by old, weathered, splintered-
with-age wood beams that held a structure up.
We were in a cramped dark space, she and I.
She asked me, heart-to-heart, if I had sympathy
for her brother who'd died in battle years ago.
I flatly, unemotionally, but honestly, said I did
not feel sympathy for her brother. But it wasn't
me who said it. Someone else was there—an
observer—and I wept because she was so hurt
by his hardness.

I was counting my money when there was a
knock on the partition.

"Come in."

It was Nick.

"You want to come down for a drink?"

"Maybe."

"We're going to have a glass of wine and
watch Jeopardy at 6:30. You like Jeopardy?"

"Everybody likes Jeopardy."

"Okay."

He disappeared back around the column.

The sun was still up. It wasn't even caught in the trees across the street yet. Too early to start drinking. I didn't even want to drink. I opened the book I'd found in front of the library.

> The storm ripped over the mountains, gushing torrents of rain that struck the ground with the sharp ring of metal on stone. Lightning strikes spat down, angry artillery fire that slammed against the cannon roar of thunder. There was a gleeful kind of mean in the air, a sizzle of temper and spite that boiled with power. It suited Mallory Price's mood perfectly.

I flipped the page.

> His eyes were midnight blue. She felt the power of them, a flash of heat along her skin, when they met hers. She wasn't a fanciful woman. Anything but, she told herself. But the storm, the house, the sheer ferocity of that gaze made her feel as though he could see everything in her mind. Everything that had ever been in her mind.

I threw that son of a bitch over the side of the balcony. It lay face open on the sidewalk, hard for someone not to stumble over. A man walked by. A woman walked by. A white man, a black woman. Two kids whose parents were from India. Nobody picked it up.

I went downstairs to throw it in the trash. The book was gone. Who'd picked it up? I looked down the sidewalk both ways. Across the street, little Nate was peaking around the corner of his apartment. He ran behind the building.

I crossed the street. He peaked out, then ran away again. I followed into the parking lot in back of the building. He threw the book at me. It bounced off my shin.

"Hiya! See ya!" he said, and ran between my legs back to the front of the building.

I decided to buy a can of Coke at the corner store.

On the way back I met Nate's dad. He was walking toward me on the left side of the sidewalk, the wrong side. I wasn't going to move for him on the principle built by western civilization that there is a right side and a wrong side, otherwise there would be chaos. We came closer and closer. He had to move, I wasn't going to. We bumped shoulders. I looked back. He didn't. He said to the air in front of him, "I'm tired of movin over for you people!"

You people?

My legs shook. Tony was an evil racist. I ran upstairs and locked the door behind me. I'd done it now. I'd gone too far. I had an enemy across the street who might attack at any time.

A friend of mine got locked in his trunk *twice*. After that, he bought a derringer and kept it under the front seat between his legs. I used to pick up anyone on the street who waved me down, but then I learned that young black men can be trouble. It wasn't something I wanted to learn. I resisted it longer than most. People who've never driven a cab say cab drivers are racist, that they think all black men are alike, but it's not like that. I met a lot of black customers and I liked them and they were fine, but ninety percent of my "no pays" were young black men. You try driving strangers around at night, with them sitting right behind you. You do that for three years and then get back to me.

Julie's apartment was thrift store magic. A tattered couch and a big chair, lots of taste and comfort. A coffee table made by a Cajun farmer out of deep green wainscoting boards. A friendly, threadbare Oriental rug. A garish painting of a crucifix hung on the wall above the couch.

Julie noticed.

"I have a *crucifixation*," she said.

To the right of Christ was a placid mountain scene, and to the left of Christ was a clown with a big teardrop on his cheek.

"I spent a hundred dollars, total," she said.

Nick came out of the bathroom carrying a book. I asked him what he was reading.

"Some science fiction thing."

Julie said, "It's not 'some science fiction thing!' It's a meta sci-fi classic! Written by none other than Philip K. Dick!"

"Never read him," I said.

"You've never read him?"

"Never read him."

She looked at me like I cut chickens into parts for a living.

"I'll borrow it to you," said Nick.

"Nick, you *lend* something to a person; you *borrow* something *from* a person," said Julie.

"I'll lend it to him then."

"That's right."

Julie said, "My goal in life is to *live* literature, not write it. Writing in our age is a secondary act. To live is the primary act."

"Who said that?"

"I did."

I wondered if she talked like that to Nick when they were alone.

"I don't experience boundaries the way other people do," she said, and she winked, I thought, but I wasn't sure.

I felt twice as likely to be abused as a single person than if I were in a relationship and there were two of us to absorb her.

Nick craned his head toward the window, pulled the curtain aside, and peeked out at the area in front of the building.

"What are you looking at?" Julie said.

"I heard a sound."

"He's always hearing sounds. He's alert, like John Cage."

Nick asked me if I wanted beer or wine.

"Whatever's easiest."

He handed me a red plastic cup with red wine in it.

"Drink up," said Julie, "That's all you can do in New Orleans—is drink up."

"I'm not much of a drinker. Two is alright, but three are too many."

"And four is a whore?"

She laughed, then coughed.

I went to the bathroom.

Nothing on their walls. Clean as a whistle. I pissed and thought of Libby, beautiful red-haired Libby. Her body was strong and healthy and real. Was there a correlation between that and her inward beauty? Why did I always assume there was? I zipped up and went back to the living room.

Julie was rooting around on the floor looking for a lost cork. I could see the tops of her breasts. I wanted to fuck them. No, I wasn't sure.

"How did you two meet?"

"By the mailboxes one morning, and by that night we were lovers. Not *in* love, but lovers. And we still are."

She smiled at Nick.

My face got red.

"What's the matter?"

I drained my red plastic cup and stood up to go. I sat down. It was way too early to exit without making a scene. Nick poured me another cup.

"Why do you keep your apartment upstairs?" I asked Nick.

"It's his escape hatch," Julie said, "in case things go to shit down here. He'll keep it as long as we're together. He's a smart boy that way. Every relationship should have an escape hatch."

But that contradicted my dream of The Outhouse and a Good Marriage. I wanted to tell them the dream.

She said, "Toronto is more like New York City than New York City. I was born in The Upper West Side, if you must know. My parents split up when I was four, and my mother took me back to Canada. Toronto is the best!"

"Better than New Orleans?"

"Clearly."

Julie turned the TV on. Alex Trebek was reading out categories. "Notable Women for 200," said a contestant.

Alex Trebek said, "This Vietnam Veterans Memorial designer was the subject of an Oscar-winning documentary."

Julie pumped her fist and said, "Maya Lin!"

"Notable Women for 400."

"NPR legal eagle Nina Totenberg reported on this woman's story, helping reopen the Clarence Thomas hearings."

Julie pumped her fist and said, "Anita Hill!"

I hadn't had a TV in six years. It was like someone I hated, but forgotten, had turned up.

Jeopardy ended, mercifully, but the TV stayed on. There was a sitcom about a fat, jolly, bland white guy and his petite, super-sexy but nagging wife, and their three sweet, impish, wise-cracking kids. Julie talked over it.

She said Canadian public television was superior to American public television. She said the state of Canada's fishing industry was corrupt, and that was why she didn't eat fish. She told me about the tar sands in Alberta and the damage that was being done to the First Nations people who lived there.

The room felt loud and messy.

I finished another cup of wine and went into the kitchen for another.

I thought Julie couldn't be blamed for the way she was, just like I couldn't be blamed for the way I was. She had an illness called Verbal Sadism. She channeled spirits through her mouth that couldn't shut up. She was possessed by a polymorphous verbal motherfucker. I had an illness too, but I had no clue what it was called. Maybe she and I could communicate yet, and become sympathetic to each other's sickness.

I filled my cup to the rim.

Julie asked me if I'd ever read *The Yellow Wall-paper*.

I said, "Yes."

I lied.

"Why did you come down to New Orleans anyway?" she said.

"To get an apartment."

"No, really."

"Really. I came down here to live in this apartment building. I've always wanted to live in *this* apartment building."

She crossed her legs and said, "Are you a writer?"

"No."

"I'm going upstairs," said Nick.

"What—you're leaving me?"

"I'll be back. I just need to take a dump."

"Romantic, isn't he?"

I asked if she ever wore shorts.

She said, "Nick does. He goes around without a shirt on a lot too. But it's illegal for me, you know."

"I can sympathize."

"Can you?"

"Probably not."

Maybe there was more to Julie than I could see on surface. Why did I always think I could see all there was to see?

"Did you know Darla?"

"I don't want to talk about Darla."

"Why not?"

"I don't want to talk about it."

"Why?"

"Because I don't want to."

Nick came back and balled himself up in the big easy chair.

"You ever do anything evil?" he said.

"I don't believe in the existence of evil," said Julie, "but I did commit a crime once. Have you ever spent a night in jail?"

"No," I said.

"I think everyone should spend at least one night in jail."

"Why?"

"My boyfriend and I stole a *USA Today* newsstand. We were living in Brooklyn at the time, and we wanted to use it as a stereo cabinet. We were going to leave the day's paper in the front window, and he was going to gut it out so we could open and close it without using quarters. It was just a fun idea, but I got caught and my boyfriend absconded."

"You took the fall," said Nick.

"That was big of me," she said.

"Bigamy," I said.

I was thinking about my crime that was too heinous and involved, and too psychologically-thick to tell. How I was guilty, but not directly. How nothing could be traced back to me. My dreams kept telling me how, as a criminal, I knew how to hide my guilt and go about my daily life undetected.

I had a dream once that a man was riding in the backseat of my cab shooting a shotgun at people coming up behind us. I ducked down and told him to duck down too, but he stayed up, shooting, as we drove out to the suburbs to pick up a shotgun for me. I fired test-shots down the highway while driving back toward the city. We came to a battlefield, and three women were descending a staircase naked, one was the first girl I'd ever kissed and I wanted to apologize to her for not being naked, then my body was trim, and I was naked too, and descending the staircase too. The war was over, and I was in the center of a city, and around a Roman-like fountain bodies were lying in clumps three-deep, decayed beyond recognition, oozing puss, and I couldn't bear to touch the body I was assigned to remove, so I dragged it by the pant leg. I was told to show respect for the dead, so I put my arm around his waist and carried him the best I could, his torso and head dangled back and to the side.

"Want some more wine?" said Nick.

"Yes, please."

Julie stubbed her cigarette out on the wooden floor and ground it in with her shoe.

"Nobody wants to die," she said. "All the top religions are based on this prejudice, and now Science is on the game too. They want to treat death like a disease, and if they ever succeed it'll mark the end of biological evolution. Mark my words, we're a dangerous bunch. Over the past ten thousand years we've fabricated an entire world that doesn't exist. And now things are accelerating at a salutatory rate."

I'd never heard that word.

And I noticed she was lifting the ends of her sentences up now, like she belonged to the aristocracy in England. And I noticed that Nick kept getting smaller and smaller, swallowed up more and more by the over-sized easy chair. I kept drinking, and holding on tight around the corners.

Julie asked for a cigarette.

"All out," said Nick.

She gave him a look that said 'you smoked the last cigarette, Nick, and you failed to replenish the supply?'

"I didn't," he said.

She groaned, "I have to get up early in the morning."

Was the party over? Was this the signal that I should leave?

"I bought the last pack, it's your turn," said Nick.

"No, I bought the last pack, it's *your* turn."

"Just go buy a pack of cigarettes, Julie."

I took a drink.

Nick left for the corner store to buy cigarettes.

Conan O'Brien was saying some bullshit to some bullshit guest. Things were coming loose in my head. Conan was meaningless. I was meaningless. And Julie seemed nervous without Nick there, or was it because she didn't have a cigarette to prop her up?

"What about James M. Cain?" I said.

"Who? The genre writer?"

"He's hard-boiled but..."

"Cain writes mysteries. He's a mystery writer. So what's the mystery?"

"He's not a mystery writer."

She laughed at her own joke, and, if she'd had a cigarette I'm sure she would've blown a column of smoke straight in my face.

"I prefer writers like Foucault, Derrida, and Lacan."

"They're full of shit."

"Now you're just being ignorant."

I moved across the room. Her intelligence and beauty and hardness made me want to kiss her. I stood in front of her. I leaned down and forward. I touched her cheek with my fingers, and said, "What do you see in Nick anyway?"

She looked away.

I backed across to my side of the room.

Had I really almost kissed her while her boyfriend was out for cigarettes?

She said, like nothing had happened, "If you hate them so much, then tell me why... Come on, state your reasons. Opinions are for the dirty masses. Come on, talk!"

I thought Foucault, Derrida and Lacan were too dense, and I'd never been able to find my way into them. Mostly I'd heard their names dropped in classrooms and at parties— like golden turds—to show how erudite, informed, and postmodern the name droppers were.

"Do you want to smoke a joint?" she said.

"No."

"Why not? It relaxes you."

"It relaxes me?"

"You seem..."

"What?"

"Like an intellectual...drifter."

She was sharp. She could kill. I had to stay on my toes. I had to be the rock to Julie's relentless, pounding waves. She reared her beautiful head and laughed.

"What's so funny?"

"You look so serious."

Nick came back with a pack of filtered Marlboros.

Julie frowned.

"That's all they had."

"You want one?" he said to me.

"No."

"They're good for you. It says so right on the book of matches." He handed me the book. I read, 'Cigarettes are addictive. Please come back every day.'

"That's very clever," I said.

Julie said, "What's the most ridiculous story you've never told?"

I said, "I had a pair of shoes three years ago, and the sole of one of them was coming off. It flopped so bad I had to lift one foot up high just to walk. I must have looked funny walking down the street, but I loved those shoes, and one shoe was like new, so I didn't want to give up on them as a pair. Then one night I was with my roommate, we were driving around trying to find a parking spot—circling and circling—and there in the middle of the street was a shoe. I jumped out of the car. It was a shoe, just like mine! Same foot, same style, right size! So I laid my old shoe down in the exact same position it'd been in and ran back to the car. I imagined two men were driving around the block, and they'd be back any second, and they'd find an old shoe where a new shoe had been a minute before!"

"Do you really expect us to believe that?" said Julie.

"But it happened."

"Right. Somebody threw a shoe out the window at the same moment you needed that exact same shoe," said Nick.

"That's what's so amazing about it!" I said.

They were giggling and taking swigs of wine from red plastic cups.

The one miraculous thing that had ever happened to me in my life and they were making fun of it.

"Oh, we're just teasing," said Julie. "We know it happened. It had to have happened. You can't make shit like that up. Isn't that right, Nick?"

"Absolutely," said Nick as he wiped tears of laughter from his eyes.

"If I were an ethnoarcheologist, and I'm not, I'd say that I've never met a person who required so much digging! And I wonder if there's a person alive who'd be up to such an excavation?"

She was trying to kill me. I breathed back retaliatory action. All while the TV kept talking. And Julie kept talking.

"So," she said, "do you want to borrow Nick's TV or not?"

"Sure."

"Do you have an ice cube tray?" said Julie.

"No."

"Do you want to borrow ours? We have an extra."

Julie led Nick and me out the door and up the stairs to Nick's apartment. Then he and I lugged the huge black and white set over to my place while Julie went downstairs to get the ice cube tray. He'd helped carry the dead dog across the street in a similar, humpbacked way. She came back up with an extension cord. We put the TV on the balcony.

The Dinner Party

There was a baby in my room and I had to help it, but I couldn't find it. I woke up, it was dark. I put my pants and socks on. Then someone was picking me up to go fishing. Nobody was picking me up. I took my clothes off and went back to bed.

I took a bike ride. It was barely light out. I pedaled hard. Nobody out but me. A piece of lined paper on the sidewalk. A handwritten letter. Who still wrote those things? Who still found those things? I sat on the curb and read.

> I got your address from my mom. I sent
> a letter last night, so this one makes 4.
> I'm tired of not hearin your voice. I hear
> you're staying in our apartment again.
> How? I'd hate to catch a case when I get
> out. I aint worried though, I know who
> my babies man is. My mom signed papers
> to drop the charges. I may get sent to
> Raleigh for a court date in June. Sign the

money orders and fill em out honey. Start
getting my letters and get a phone plz.
I'm using somebodys indegent stamps
cause I'm cashed out. Fuck I miss my
"K." Keep writing, it keeps my heart up.
I'm so proud of my "K" for taking care of
business. That's good Shit baby. I put it on
my life I'll marrie you. I miss your body.
It wont be to much longer. This just made
us stronger, don't you think? Shit I'm
whole and complete with you. You're that
women, (My women). Well its count time
so I'll end it here. Baby drop what ever you
can in cash so I can get stamps try to get
a Obamaphone So we can talk. I love you
ALWAYS and everyday that ends in Y and
its always K-DAY xoxo
P.S Imagine we're at the beach and we're
having good slow conversation suddenly a
plain flys over saying "K" will You marrie
me? I pull out the ring slide it on your
hand as I begin to softly kiss your lips
slowly making love to you. I♥U Xoxo
P.S Baby I got hard dick and bubble gum and
I'm fresh out of bubble gum...I'm ready to eat
your pussy and make love to you I love You
Dorthy Katrina Wombles. XOXO

Found on the sidewalk. Thrown down,
for sure. She definitely wasn't into it, and his
patience was going to be tried. That's what
was on trial—his patience. The desperate
undertone he was making light of—not good.
Affectionate words sandwiched between
instructions, accusations, and facts—easily
seen through.

All men have a tendency to make plans and vows and to believe in the "one"—*especially when they're in jail.*

She threw the letter down.

I biked to the library downtown. A big, not beautiful building. On the front steps, a man sucked his pinky finger, then put it in his ear. He held a cell phone up to his other ear. "Sure it's me, who did you think it was?"

A man shelving books seemed calm, like the library was a contemplative place to work. Maybe I'd want to be a librarian one day. A sexy woman sat at a table nursing a book. Her breasts were covered in a thin layer of cotton that ran horizontally an eighth of an inch above her nipples that were as hard as rope knots. Did my male ancestors think like this?

Back on my bike, I rode north. I'd never been up that way. Midtown, Mid City, whatever it's called. Broad Street. Ugly. A brick building with two enormous pipes coming out the side, each pipe (freshly painted green) ten feet across and curved mightily, like the backs of killer whales, down into the ground. I rode past them, puzzled.

Fingers laced through chain link fencing. Dull, watery eyes staring out. I crossed the street to the other side to get away from the black men dressed in orange jump suits. Five gymnasium-sized Quonset-like tents. A vacant lot turned into a jail. Too many criminals? Too much crime? Not enough tax base? All young, all black, all men. Each had caught a case, but did they have bubble gum? Tonight would each man write a letter to his girlfriend that he'd cheated on, but now depended on, and envisioned as the queen of his soul?

I went into a dark bar to have a drink. I ordered a Coke. I found a place to stand. A baby in a highchair was the center of attention. Its mom and dad and a group of friends were gathered around it. The baby pointed, and said, "Wow!" and cheers went up from a group of young men drinking at a table nearby. The baby turned to look, and the young men became wide-eyed and shy. I laughed loud enough for the baby to hear me, and it turned to look. I smiled. It smiled. The mom and dad smiled. I didn't have a disease. I could love a child. Two of the young men at the table nearby began to play peek-a-boo with the baby. Birthday presents were put in front of it. I loved them all.

Outside in the bright sun, I farted. I let go of what I'd been holding in without thinking about it. It began to sprinkle. It smelled wonderful, then a heavy downpour. I rode home, got soaked.

Nick and Julie's curtains were closed. I could see the ghost of TV light flickering through the curtain. My idiot savant, shut-in neighbors. I tiptoed past.

I sat on the balcony and waited for a knock on the partition. I waited an hour. I waited two hours. I began to feel secure. I began to miss them. I didn't want to see them. There was a knock on the partition.

"You want to come down? We're having a dinner party," said Nick.

"A dinner party? Sure. When?"

"In about an hour."

Because I needed a place to go. Against my better judgment, I needed them. Though they'd treated me badly, and I was invisible. I had Nick's TV. I had Julie's ice cube tray and extension cord. I imagined this time would be different. They were having a dinner party. There would be guests. Dinner parties could be fun. I might meet someone. Maybe a lover. All the moments of tedium and hogwash and pig shit were leading up to a beautiful moment? I could always leave. I wouldn't take shit from them. I'd take the lead in conversation. The shoe story—my one true, fabulous, unique, singular impossible story—and they'd ruined it. My gut hurt. My head hurt. Even my hair, though short, started to worry.

I took a shower in the green water. I crouched naked in the French doorway, afraid of being seen by Nick on the other side of the partition, or by Tony across the street. I looked off to the left to see what my old friends the happy cracker family were up to.

They were either inside the house or at a bingo palace, but I wanted to see them playing checkers and squirting hoses. So I dressed them up. I put summer dresses on the fat women and made them thin. I put the old man and young man in new blue jeans. I stood them outside a white church in the country, and had them square dance on the lawn.

But they knew I'd put them there. They saw how they were being made to represent people that my mother and father had probably known and loved and lost. They scowled at me. It wasn't fun for them to square dance for me. They stopped.

To punish them I turned them into non-thinking sea anemones asleep in a dark gelatinous seabed at the bottom of the ocean, kept down forever by the earth's pressure.

Nick and Julie were watching a TV sitcom when I came in. Just the two of them. I didn't smell any food cooking.

"Where's the dinner party?"

"*Shit* down and take a load off," said Nick.

Julie didn't look up from the TV.

Had I become a member of their dysfunctional family? Was I the third wheel they needed to keep their sad little tricycle rolling? I'd seen this kind of behavior before, when a TV is the crucial element to whatever is missing in people's lives, so it can't be turned off without raising a silence nobody would want to hear.

They laughed at punch lines that weren't funny, triggered by canned laughter that I thought they were too smart to fall for. The sitcom ended, then a new show started, a hospital drama that I thought was funnier than the sitcom, but Nick and Julie glared at me every time I laughed. When it ended, the TV stayed on.

"How about we go to Café du Monde to see how the other half lives," I said.

"No," said Julie, "let's go to the Economy Bar."

"The Economy is closed for the summer, no AC," I said.

"I have an idea," said Nick, "Let's go to a place nobody's ever been to, or even heard of. We'll just go to...a place!"

I wondered if the place no one had been to, or even heard of, would have food.

I didn't pay attention on the way, and I didn't look at the sign for the place when we went in, and while we were in there I didn't ask, so afterward I didn't know where we'd been. We sat on stools next to three sad drunks slumped over at the bar, and I guessed it was cool to be close to them.

Nick said, "Mike, Mike, Mike."

I looked at him.

"My name is Mike and I ride a bike. I live on Magazine Street and I have no feet."

"That's pretty good. I hear you write poetry."

"Just for fun. To kill time. To rhyme. When it comes to me."

"There's a booth," said Julie. We took our beers and followed. "A booth is nicer," she said.

We drank our Miller High Lifes in silence quickly, like we needed to be somewhere else. We drove back to Nick and Julie's place. I helped Nick lug a cooler, case of beer, and a bag of ice in. We set the cooler down in the middle of the living room floor. This was their idea of a dinner party? We popped open three fresh cans. Julie went into the bedroom and came back out wearing a flannel shirt.

"So what do you do when you work?" Julie asked me.

"Cab driver."

"Oh, you drive a cab? That must be interesting."

Like I hadn't told her before.

"It's not."

"Did you go to college?" she said.

"Yes."

"What did you study?"

"Law."

"Are you serious?"

"No."

"It sure is hot tonight," Nick said.

"I would whither if I had to live up on the top floor."

"They're forecasting rain."

I went to the bathroom.

Julie said, "I went to an exotic dance club in Toronto once with my former boyfriend, and was it risqué!"

"What's so risqué about a strip joint?" I said.

"'Exotic dance club,'" is the appropriate term. And what do you mean, it's not risqué? A girl opened her legs four inches from my face, and I saw into her twat!"

"Did you have your clothes on?"

"I don't want to argue."

I took a slug of beer.

"Strip clubs are designated places for risqueness to occur, so whatever happens there is, by definition, not risqué. Men pay women for services rendered. Women get on stage and men pay to watch. It'd be risqué if everyone in the audience took off their clothes, or if they eliminated the stage all together and took the money out of the equation."

I was pretty articulate, and Julie didn't rebut, so I went on.

"The women are pretty. The men are ugly. The women are naked. The men have their pants on. The men pay. The women get paid. Nobody's naked. Taking your clothes off doesn't make you naked. We'd all like to be naked, but it's not that easy."

"You seem to know quite a bit about exotic dance clubs."

"I drove a cab. I saw a lot. Strip clubs remind me of dogs barking behind locked doors. The owners are dead, but the dogs don't know it, so they keep barking. They're hungry and they want to be fed, so they'll go on barking until they die."

This seemed to make Julie sad, like I'd touched a raw nerve. I was on a roll.

"A lot of men who go to strip clubs have wives at home that they've fucked too many millions of times. There's no more juice in it, so strip clubs are there to siphon off the excess juice. And most of the women who dance in strip clubs? They have a kid or two at home—that's who they're really dancing for."

Was I coming on too strong? I didn't care.

"Men have no idea what it's like to be a sex object. That's why it's so easy for them to ogle, look at, take and fuck anything that moves that's cute. Because nobody ogles, looks at, takes or fucks them."

"So you want to get on a stage and dance naked, is that it?"

I didn't answer.

I said, "I asked Colette once if I was beautiful, and you know what she said? Well, first she laughed, and then she said, 'Of course not. What a ridiculous question.' It was like I hadn't learned this basic fact of life, as a boy, and she had to teach me. It was so depressing."

"Who's Colette?" said Nick.

Julie said, "I wasn't talking about *frequenting* exotic dance clubs, I was talking about *a* single visit, with my *boyfriend*, as an *experiment*. Besides, you seem to be saying much more about your sexuality than perhaps you're aware of."

I'd been judged. And in order to be un-judged I would've had to argue. And to argue I would've had to gather my thoughts in one place and lay them out in order.

"You're saying that women are objectified, but that's a given," said Julie. "That's old news. What new can you bring to the table?"

She unwrapped the cellophane from a fresh pack of unfiltered American Spirits, and tamped the end of the box—tamp, tamp, tamp—against the heel of her palm—tamp, tamp, tamp—like this was a scientifically proven method for bringing the utmost flavor and best smoke out of a cigarette.

"The way I see it..." she said.

"Why does it always have to be the way *you* see it?"

I'd shouted.

The walls had flattened out, and the room had gone into outer space.

Where was I?

Julie was looking at Nick, and Nick was looking at Julie.

I stood up.

A mean violent stranger had burst into their living room. I clenched his fists and my legs shook.

Or was that what they wanted? For me to lose it? Were they so bored and dead inside they needed me to ride their tiny tricycle around the room for awhile and then crash, and then afterward they could be alone again and talk about the crazy guy who lived upstairs?

I staggered out.

Fuck me
I am a Cunt
I don't Ever Want to See You again

Noted Ventriloquist

I heard the big tree swishing in front of the apartment and I smelled soft rain coming. I didn't dare go onto the balcony though, even to cry. I lay sprawled on the dirty bedroom floor. I'd been gotten to. I had enemies in the building. Why couldn't I argue in moderation? Why couldn't I accept disagreement with grace? Why did I have to speak my mind? Why couldn't I recognize them for the fucked up people they were?

Did I want to strip?

I ran a butcher knife through Julie's ribs and curled up to sleep. I didn't come down to New Orleans for this. Had she made the hermit story up to bait me? Had she got the idea from my bathroom walls? Why would someone so beautiful, with such fine features and smooth hands, be so cruel? I stabbed her in the forehead with the rustiest nail I could think of. Then I heard a motorcycle starting up.

I ran to the balcony.

Julie was walking out of the building, getting on the back of a motorcycle. She was wearing a black leather jacket and a shiny black helmet. I didn't know Nick had a motorcycle. She put her arms around his leather waist. Her long hair flew behind as they sped off.

I pretended I had no arms. I was a man with no arms. I let my bike run into the bumper of a parked car. I'd been born with three arms, and I operated life on the assumption that one day I'd have my missing arm back. A pretty young woman rode by, rang her cute thumb bell at me as I sat on the curb.

I was in the French Quarter before I knew it. The wind blew me there in the fragrant drizzle. The nighttime buzz of fake American seediness. Hayseeds inhaling debauchery on three-day-weekends. Drunken, white-legged, plain-faced folks from the Midwest strolling around with plastic beer cups in their hands. Clean-cut Des Moinian boys with vomit on their shoes, asking girls to flash their tits for beads. A canned experience, and the locals played their parts too.

I locked my bike to a street light and went through a door. The bar was u-shaped. A man sitting on a barstool fifteen feet across from me had a woman between his legs. She was standing, aiming her conversation sideways at a girlfriend. Her mouth was moving, nothing else. I stared at them instead of taking a swig of gin and tonic. His hand caressed her wooden lower back.

"A noted ventriloquist," I said, "and his famous dummy."

Her long hair flipped around and slapped him in the face. The audience laughed. I watched his hand to see how the trick was done. It swept back and forth, then slowly lowered and settled on the crack of her ass. She didn't turn around, or shudder, or acknowledge in any way that someone's fingers were on the crack of her ass. She kept talking sideways to her girlfriend. I noticed a translucent orange glow coming from the soft cartilage of her ear. The ventriloquist didn't see what I saw. To him, she was just wood. But the bar light was shining through her ear, for me! If she were mine, I would've said, "We are flesh and blood mammals, pulsating on this green earth, kiss me!"

I looked over at what he was looking at: a woman wearing a short green dress with large black X's on it was shooting pool on the other side of the room, rubbing a well-chalked pool cue back and forth between her fingers. My head swiveled back to the ventriloquist. His hand on the dummy's back had come back to life. It was traveling along, around, and up and down— looking for what? The heart string? The string that he could pull to make her face turn and kiss him? I looked back to the woman playing pool.

She'd taken her shot and was standing erect, chalking her stick, talking to a friend. She was beautifully-carved and sanded down by generations of conscious social breeding. Courtly gentlemen had married refined and fine-looking maidens down through the centuries to make her.

The bartender said, "You don't look so good."

Because everyone was happy but I wasn't. Because they were all productive and I wasn't. Or did I look happy and productive to them? People always seemed surprised when I got around to telling them how miserable I was. Maybe everyone seemed fine. Maybe that was evolution's talent, or trick—to make us all appear well when we weren't, so we'd envy each other, and assume the other was happier and more productive than we were.

A man sat down next to me. A talker. I could've been Jesus Christ himself, and he would've talked and not listened.

"I hit two homeruns in one inning in a high school baseball game. Nobody ever does that," he said.

"That's amazing," I said.

"The wind was blowing out."

"You're selling yourself short."

"No, the wind was blowing hard, straight out to center field."

"But you hit two homeruns in one inning, man. Nobody ever does that!"

"But the wind...you see, the wind. Everyone always teases me when I tell them about the wind. They think I'm exaggerating. That I did this great thing and won't own up to it. But it's a fact. The wind was blowing out like a motherfucker."

"I believe you. You didn't do shit. It was all the wind."

"That's right."

When he went to the bathroom I skipped out.

Julie had asked me if I wanted a cigarette. I'd said no. But she didn't know if I'd meant, "No, I don't want a cigarette right now," or "No, I don't smoke," or "No, I don't smoke filtered cigarettes." She'd been too busy tamping her fucking filtered cigarettes and flipping through her fucking index file of things to say next.

I shouted down the length of Bourbon Street, "I don't smoke anything that has a right and a wrong end!"

After walking a mile in God knows whose shoes, or in what direction, I hailed a taxi. She looked at me like I'd better not vomit in her cab. I told her I wanted to get out. I paid the fare and didn't tip. Fuck her. I thought of Libby, and fumbled in my back pocket for her number. No, better not call. Not good to slur into a telephone. What was the name of that bar she worked at? My eyes felt winded and out of breath.

Why had I never learned to act? If I'd become an actor, I would've been able to be different people at different times. But I didn't know how to act. I wore the same face all the time, everywhere I went. It must have been sewn on me by the time I was ten. Had I ever played like the boys on the raft, making it up as I went? Drunk on some random street in New Orleans, I scolded myself: Act!

I went into a bar. I came out of a bar. A car ignition ignited. A horse and carriage clopped by. The invented world, not just Bourbon Street, but everywhere, had penetrated me long ago—as it had all unsuspecting children—and made me believe the things that appeared before me were real.

I wanted to show up on Libby's doorstep. Good thing I didn't know where she lived. Better to bar hop. I sat down in a joint. I ordered a beer and a shot of whiskey and stared at them. I noted the deceptive shape of the neck of the beer bottle after I'd poured its contents into a glass.

A man said, "My ultimate task is to bridge the different intellectual worlds."

He was going to do what?

He quoted Nietzsche. "'It is out of the deepest depths that the highest must come to its height.'"

I didn't care for his earnestness, and I tipped the bartender who wasn't even there, five dollars, and left.

Bridges are a shitty business. They go over nature's natural limitations and take us to places we don't need to go. We're not bridges. We're rafts, if we're lucky.

Breasts and nipples barely hidden under cotton and linen bobbed up and down on Bourbon Street. "Get your ass in my bed, so I can lick your clit!" I said outloud to no one in particular. I had to piss, but there wasn't a place to piss, so I pissed in the doorway of a closed shop. Not the designated place for pissing. I was making progress in my acting career.

Two in the morning, I snuggled into Snug Harbor. A bar without windows, dollar bills and corks hanging from the ceiling and glued to the walls. I think it was Snug Harbor. I sat down next to a beer.

"Hello beer, how's it going?"

"Fine. And you?"

"Just dandy."

"You don't look so good," said a waitress.

"I have a headache."

"You look like you're dying, actually."

She was sad, and funny, and I loved her.

"There's a drugstore on Canal Street, you should go there."

"What kind of a waitress are you?"

She smiled, showing a mouthful of metal braces. Her mouth closed carefully. She wasn't beautiful. I felt sorry for thinking that. Colette said I didn't have a soul. I said to her, "Because there's no such thing as souls! When the brain dies, we die! You can't fly away on the magic carpet of a soul just because you want to!" That was about the time she began being mean to me.

The waitress came back and handed me four Ibuprofens. I thanked her from the bottom of my heart. Too much, you know, like a drunk. She was someone's sweet daughter, someone's dear babysitter, and I'd entered into her beautiful life for a sliver of time and was blathering. I asked her out on a date. "This isn't me," I slurred. I left ten dollars and went out.

A ghost boy in line behind me at a Krystal Burgers said, "I sometimes see myself as an old person who'll regret. I don't want to be on my deathbed full of regrets."

The ghost girl standing in line beside him said, "I just want to be glad I made the choices I made. Sure, I wish I'd done some things differently but..."

My turn in line.

"I'll have a bag of hamburgers."

"Will that be all?"

"It's food, isn't it?"

I was serious.

"It's food, isn't it?"

A blinking sign said, "Everyone Welcome!" A door jingled. Three sets of eyes glared at me. I spun around, tripped on a piece of lint, pulled myself off the floor with great difficulty, and left through the jingling door.

Colette liked to beat on kitchen pots and pans at parties, and she often exposed her breasts around the house because it was natural—and this was revealing to me. So revealing, so pure, that I wondered if she was the healer I'd been waiting my whole life for. The one who didn't accept the lies that ruled our time and place. I missed her. Even when I was with her, I missed her.

Three a.m. joint stuffed with three a.m. dumb asses and other types with no tomorrows and no one but themselves to listen to both sides of their mouths flapping. I went to find my bike. Where had I parked it? Someone had stolen it? It was so windy it seemed a tree might fall on me, and I'd be discovered beneath a tree, and Colette would probably say, "Knowing him, he walked under it on purpose."

Subway sandwiches are so boring and bland and nondescript that I had to slip potato chips in to add crunch. I tried to give him ten extra dollars, but the kid wouldn't take it. I vomited and fell off my bike. I'd found my bike. It landed on top of me, and I had a hard time getting it off. A middle-aged married couple looked down at me lying on the sidewalk and the man half of the couple said, "Slob." The vomit in my mouth tasted like shit mixed with sugar.

"You ride like you gotta take a shit!" shouted a college-age jock. I pulled over to beat him up. I had the impulse to kill him, strip him naked, and turn him upside down and make his asshole do the talking. But upon closer inspection he was beefy, so I decided to stay on my bike and threaten him from a distance.

"What did you say?" I said.

"I said, 'You ride like you gotta take a shit!'"

"What if your mother heard you talking like that?"

"Fuck my mother!"

I put my dukes up and almost crashed. He ran at me like a middle linebacker. I pedaled away quickly.

I broke a beer bottle over the sidewalk's head and foam poured out like fresh cement.

I woke up in a park. Something was loud. A mosquito. I felt sorry for it, and didn't kill it. I hated life. I didn't ask to be born. I hated flowers. I didn't see the point of buying flowers in a grocery store and giving them to a girl. Why did anyone like flowers? I'd tagged after Colette like a dog. Five mosquitoes were ganging up on my face. I let them. I wanted to be a mosquito. A lowly, indestructible one. A million light years away from "barber" "bike" and "Julie." To live and not care what the fuck it means. Fuck love, fuck words. I'd make a film from the point of view of a mosquito. I'd tell all its little secrets. What it's like to not need to understand why. What it's like to not present a theory of the world while being able to eat food more foul than nine-tenths of Lacan's best thoughts. What it's like to end up a blood smear on a salty, hairy arm. Colette was a mosquito. I was a mosquito. Nick and Julie were mosquitoes. Everyone was a mosquito. From an airplane taking off things look small, and from 50,000 feet they disappear. It's not something they teach you in school—how things disappear. Just because a mosquito can't stand in front of a classroom and lecture doesn't mean it's not a human. "Look, you mosquitoes." Dozens were walking over my face and arms and legs. "See how beautiful I am? See my sweating, trying to be worried hair? See my commitment to the destruction of the human face? You can have it all."

I must've fallen asleep because I woke up. I was under an ornate lamp post. I heard an ambulance flashing. A disaster close to someone, right inside the guts of someone else. I heard a newspaper rustling. A worn and pock-marked newspaper had traveled all day to meet me. I somehow climbed on my bike. I climbed on my bike somehow, very carefully. I tried three times to trap the newspaper under my front tire. I braked hard and somersaulted, pounded down on my back. My thoughts were sucked out as I writhed and tried to breathe. I reached my right arm out like a crane, across my belly, and brought the newspaper in. Yesterday's paper. Way back then! I rolled over onto my stomach and flattened it out.

On the front page was an article about Nicaraguans who were making $1.48 a day (women $1.11) at a coffee plantation that had failed because The World Bank and the French government had created a coffee industry in Vietnam that was now second to Brazil, which had deflated prices worldwide, so these poor Nicaraguan families were out of work. There was a picture of adults holding children, and teenage daughters standing sad-faced. They'd walked three days in the mountains where they said they were so high the clouds were below them, to get to this city where they'd slept in a public park and were now waiting for someone to help them. And we think bringing children into the world requires planning, a certain amount of income, a certain level of education, and a certain size of house. I shed a gush of tears for the Nicaraguans.

Dawn was coming up like a red rose blooming. It was going to be a fine morning for someone. My neck hurt, my shoulders ached, my temples throbbed. I had to hit the road. I had to go. I meandered down a wide street. Meander is a river in Turkey. I saw lights coming on. People were getting out of bed, getting dressed, going to work. The tar on the street was black, smooth, and freshly laid. A street sign said Elysian Fields. I passed a long row of cars that people were sleeping in. I kept pedaling. A train whistle blew in the distance. I rode to the river, slowly, slowly, slowly, five miles.

A boy standing on the shore was holding a fishing pole. He had the whole, dark, wide, brown river to himself. If I knew how to swim I would've abandoned my bike and swum across the Mississippi to Algiers where everything would've been different.

A light was on in Nick and Julie's apartment. The curtain was open. Julie was sitting in the big chair, reading. She'd either gotten out of bed early, or she hadn't gone to bed yet. Was she studying to be a professor? Was that why she talked the way she did? Was she practicing on me? She might make it, for all I knew. Maybe she'd become a brilliant professor one day. But for now all she could do was talk. And anybody can talk.

Blow It Up

A woman was sleeping with me but she didn't have a pillow, so I fluffed mine up and put it under her head. In the morning, my pillow lay alone on the other side of the bed.

I had swollen red circles up and down my arms and legs. My face was covered. I licked them and itched them carefully, not wanting to make blisters. Not knowing what to do, I went out to the balcony.

Tony and two white guys were standing in front of the apartment building across the street. The white guys were young and preppy-looking, and they kept pointing at the mess in front of the apartment. Tony nodded like he was on it. They put their hands on their hips. Tony nodded that he understood. Tony was the caretaker, clearly, and those two suburban fucks owned the apartment.

After the white guys left, Tony opened a couple of windows and turned the music up loud, and his friends streamed out to the front of the building where they stood and smirked. A real Uncle Tom, that Tony.

I was filling my cab up with gas at the end of a shift at two in the morning, when four black girls came up asking for a ride. I said I'd take them, but I had to call the dispatcher first, in case another cab was on its way. I waited to get in on the dispatch line.

I said, "You did call a cab, right?"

"Yeah," they said.

"A Red & White?"

"Yeah, your company."

"Where from? Here? The phone booth?"

"No, from a house over there."

"Which house?"

"One down the street, mother fucker!"

"I'm not going to take you, forget it."

"You fucker! I'm gonna bash your head up!"

They were high, drunk and cold, and they believed in their hearts I was dissing them, which was bullshit. One of the girls came right up to my face, ready to hit me. The others ganged up around me. I thought, "Fuck, are they going to beat me up, these girls?"

"Why you dis us, Nigger?"

Then the girl who'd done the talking at first showed a reflective side of her personality. She said, "Maybe you had a long hard day, but you shouldn't treat others like shit you know."

I ignored them and pumped gas.

A Yellow Cab pulled up to the phone booth, and they ran over and it scooped them up. I yelled, "Liars! Fucking god damn lying sons of bitches!"

The old Greek, or Turkish, or Lebanese man who worked behind the bullet-proof glass of the locked Amoco station shook his head, and I shook mine. I put money on the tray and he slid it back in.

But the night before I'd been rude to him, when I'd wanted tortilla chips but not the kind he held up, and he'd had to hop around because my view was blocked by this and that, and he kept picking up things I didn't want, until by accident he hit on the right item.

Now we were on the same side.

I could never predict when the raging fire of racial mistrust would jump its fence and burn a hole in me.

Nick knocked on the front door. He stood in the hall.

"What happened to your face?"

"Nothing."

"Julie's been crying. She feels really bad."

I looked at him with dull, watery eyes. I itched my arm.

"She gives off a vibe when you meet her, but when you get to know her..."

"She's fucked up, Nick."

"No she's not."

I licked my finger and touched a mosquito bite on my cheek.

"She's fucked up, I'm sorry," I said.

"You two are a lot alike, you know."

"Hell we are!"

"She's actually a good listener, if you... A lot of good friends of hers were turned off at first."

"She told you that?"

"Yeah, but she's sweet. She's really..."

I closed the door and scratched my face.

I took the number 11 bus at night to Napoleon Avenue. At the bus stop a small black woman, or girl, wanted to do something for me. She held a squeegee in her hand. Didn't she see that I'd just got off the bus?

"Do you want stuff?"

"No."

"I'll do something for you."

"No."

She lifted her jacket to show me her belly.

"You want to come with me?"

I gave her a dollar.

"That's not enough. Let's do it."

"That's not enough?"

I grabbed my dollar back.

"I get a dollar all the time. I'm hungry!"

I walked past her, angry.

"A dollar don't make up to nothin!"

She followed me and my white money down the block toward Tipitina's, a barn of a music hall, where I was going. I looked back and she was gone.

The cover charge was five bucks, so I stood outside, leaned up against the brick wall to catch the vibe. Loud, hammering R&B, some swamp rock thing.

Employed people sat on the grass in the median, around two fat palm trees. Their lives had purpose and meaning. They were interesting and interested. They were half drunk, not fully drunk. They liked laughing, talking and sitting cross-legged on the grass.

A hand touched my elbow and a voice asked me to sit down with them. I'd almost forgot how. She had a feminine body and a fresh face. Someone lit a joint and passed it around. I passed, and she passed. She laughed, I laughed. She asked me if I wanted to take a walk.

We stopped under a moss-hanging tree and kissed. We sat in a doorway and touched. I kissed her neck. She rubbed her hands over my thighs. She said her name was Ellen, and she was a mom with two kids who'd recently separated from her husband, and her friends had taken her out on the town to take her away from it all. She was unhappy, but happy to have met me. She smiled that she was sorry, but she had to get back to her friends.

"Can I call you?"

"No."

"Why not? I like kids."

"It wouldn't be a good idea."

She felt sad seeing how sad I was, so we kissed again. We started over again. We crushed each other's mouths. We rubbed each other's thighs. We stroked each other's skin. We were like magic lanterns that wanted to light up.

"I'm sorry, but my friends are waiting."

"Stay, please."

"I can't."

"Don't go."

"I have to."

She said she lived in Gretna, on the other side of the river. We held hands like teenage kids. She started to cry. We hugged. She said her life was sad, and she began to laugh. I understood why she started sentences and stopped them before she got to the end. It was useless to talk.

"Being the only adult in the house with two kids can be hell."

She kissed my forehead.

I hugged her goodbye in front of her friends who were waiting patiently, then Ellen disappeared, not little by little, but all at once. Finding her, and losing her on the same night was awful.

I whispered, "Your phone number?"

"No."

I passed the same black girl, or woman, who I'd given a dollar to and taken it back from. She was standing in the same place by the bus stop, like she hadn't moved in four hours.

"Do you want stuff?"

"No!"

"I'll do something for you."

"No!"

She lifted her jacket to show me her belly again.

"You want to come with me?"

"No! And where's your squeegee anyway?"

"My what?"

"Forget it!"

She followed me as I paced around the bus stop area.

"You want to come with me?"

"I'll give you money for the bus if you go away!" I said.

"I don't want money for the bus. Come with me."

"I don't want to!"

"Let's do it."

"Okay."

I followed her along dark streets. I had time to change my mind, but she was cute, and she needed the money, and my cock was still hard from Ellen, and I kept thinking, "The way to blow it up is to bring it to a head! The way to blow it up is to bring it to a head!"

We came to a small house with a porch full of junk. Inside, I bumped into a chair and tripped over a toy that squeaked. I smelled rotten diapers. She was a mother. She turned on the ceiling light, shoved a bunch of junk off the couch, and we sat down. I didn't care if a violent man came out from behind a door and jumped me. I didn't give a fuck.

I was thinking about Darla and restraining orders, and how can the government be expected to restrain a man from his own disaster? And how all the social workers Darla ever had were probably white women.

"How much?"

"Twenty."

"For what?"

"What you want?"

"I'd like to feel your breasts and take my pants down."

She pulled up her cotton t-shirt and black acrylic bra, exposing her little breasts. She was small. Her frame was small. She assisted with my belt and zipper and grabbed my cock, too fast.

"I'll come easy, just touch my legs."

She did.

I sucked her titties.

"Touch my balls."

She complied.

"Put your finger in my asshole."

She complied.

She was friendly and sweet.

"How old are you?"

"Twenty-one."

I wondered about that.

She pulled her finger out of my cunt and jacked me off until I came.

I'd been kissing sweet Ellen less than an hour before, and now there was slime from a prostitute on my lap.

"Are you married?"

"No."

"Does the father help support the kid?"

"He's in jail."

I let it drop.

"He's Thomas Jones, the serial rapist."

I was shocked. Thomas Jones's name and mugshot were all over the TV and newspapers. I'd just been jacked off by the girlfriend of New Orleans's most notorious serial rapist. My mouth had suckled where his mouth had suckled. It was too monstrous to imagine. And such a nice girl too. A mom.

She said she'd been shocked too, when she learned that the father of her child was a serial rapist. She thought it'd been going on when they were together. They were together for four months. He was rough sometimes, but he had a nice family. "I fainted when I saw his picture and heard his name on TV. My baby will never find out."

I knew I'd never tell anyone. A version might come out one day, about how I'd met an infamous rapist's girlfriend, probably in my cab, but the fact that I'd paid twenty dollars for her to jack me off? No, I'd leave that part out.

A Jilted Man

A jilted man was about to cut off his own head, and a group of people gathered around to watch. His kid, a five-year-old boy, wanted to watch too, but I held him back. I said, "You can't see that!"

The late morning sun streamed through the stuck window. Eighty-five degrees already, and humid. I moved slowly. Things moved slowly. Palm trees, cicadas, doves, lizards, crickets and mockingbirds all stood still. I didn't have a fan. I wasn't going to live there long enough to buy a fan. The table wobbled.

I stood on the balcony, and looked across the street. I took the garbage out. I rode my bike to an air-conditioned record store in the French Quarter. I didn't buy anything. I rode Uptown to the air-conditioned student union. I didn't buy anything. I went to an air-conditioned matinee, *Crash*, and walked out early

because of all the god damn operatic coinci-
dences.

I walked slowly past people who were
walking their dogs slowly. I looked slowly into
waste baskets, trash cans, and dumpsters in
search of letters meant for others.

I took the ferry over to Gretna. I found it
lacking, and what were the chances of running
into sweet, sad, creamy-skinned Ellen, and her
brood of beautiful children?

I ran to a pay phone that worked. I dialed
fast, before I could change my mind. A man
answered.

"I'll get her."

I waited.

I'd waited a month and a half to call her,
and now, on my last week in New Orleans, I'd
gone and done it. I was nervous, and ready to
hear she was busy.

She said she was glad that I'd finally
called. She was getting worried. But she was
half way out the door, on her way to work, at
Pat O'Brien's, did I want to come by? It was
Tuesday, so it'd be slow.

I could almost smell the scent of her long
red hair coming through the telephone.

I said, "Sure."

With generosity sprouting from my heart I hailed a bus. The passengers were beautiful. It was partly cloudy, but I wasn't rooting for one or the other. It poured and I walked in a flooded gutter. It was fun to get soaked. The air-conditioning in PJ's made me chuckle. I looked funny—dripping and grinning—as I took a seat in the courtyard just as the sun came out. My old friend. Things were blistering hot, and fine.

A graduate student was eating a muffin slowly while she carried on a sweet conversation. I found her muffin so lovely I went inside to buy myself a muffin. Colette found me negative. She felt I was a drag on her joy. But I could find a muffin lovely. There was nothing wrong with me.

People were tripping and landing in each other's laps all over the place. I walked up a woman's legs with my eyes and dreamed of the creamy center where her thighs joined. Ah, but I was thinking of Libby.

A young man approached two friends (a man and a woman) from behind, and he draped his arms around them, and said to the woman, "You're as sweet as a lily in the field." Then he turned to the man and said, "And you've been eating garlic!" They laughed.

I loved them.

I went into what was, without a doubt, the tiniest restaurant in Louisiana. Two tables. The outside area, though, was huge. The cook waited on me, then he cooked my food, and brought it out. He was the owner too. A Portobello Panini, an extravagance, because I was happy. Juicy and messy, and full of sweet, peppery flavor.

Two young men and two young women, dressed like tennis pros, sat down in the bright sun. One (a woman) had just got back from Europe, and was saying there was a guy over there who wouldn't eat any food unless it was American. In Spain, fish comes with its head and tail on, but he wouldn't touch it because he said he would have the memory of the fish's face in his mind forever. His behavior appalled her. Then a yellow jacket buzzed around her head and a stricken look came over her face. She didn't say a word, just picked up her plate and walked inside. Her friends looked at each other, picked up their plates, and followed her in.

But I didn't condemn the young woman who'd condemned the young man who'd condemned the fish-eating practices of the Spaniards. I was above that.

The cook, waiter, dishwasher, and owner came outside and took my money. Then it began to sprinkle while the sun was shining, and he said, "Two monkeys must be getting married."

I'd never heard that before.

He said it was an African saying.

I was in the right place at the right time to hear something I'd never heard before. I'd always thought there should be something to say when it's raining while the sun is shining.

The sun was shining, the trees were glistening, and a young guy with long hair, gelled and styled, wearing a t-shirt with a picture of a melting smiley face emoji and the words, "Have a Nice Trip" below it, was talking on his cell phone.

But I didn't mind.

The world wasn't perfect.

"You don't understand," he said, "She hates babies. She absolutely hates them." One of his elbows was propped on a book, *Advanced Calculus*. He was studying to be an engineer. He'd had a learning disability as a child. His father had helped him many long hours at night when he felt stupid. Then he'd got his grades up, and now look at him, drowning in personal problems.

I walked through Tulane Medical Center. Odd, it had a McDonald's on the ground floor that served fatty fast-food to future heart attack victims in the neighborhood. I ordered an order of small fries and watched an overweight man, easily three times my size, gasping for breath over a liver-pink tray littered with empty food wrappers. Then he yawned, loud and roaring, like a lion who'd just eaten a gazelle. He yawned again. He yawned like he was alone in his house. He yawned like he owned the world. He yawned like an unconscious man. But I didn't hate. He stood up and I noticed he walked with a cane. He could barely move. His hands trembled. He'd be dead soon. I felt sorry for him, and myself for being so judgmental.

I found a Wrigley's Spearmint gum wrapper on the sidewalk. I picked it up in disgust, then saw that there was a message written on the inside of the foil wrapper, like a fortune cookie, but more interesting than a fortune cookie because it was unexpected.

"Pick up your trash!"

That pissed me off, but then I got over it and carried that gum wrapper five, maybe six blocks until I came to a garbage can. My rule of thumb normally was that if I didn't come to a trash receptacle within one block it was trash again. If only someone had been there filming me.

I came up to a man harnessed to a sandwich board that read "The end of the world is nigh." I stopped to talk to him.

"Why 'nigh'?"

"It means 'near.'"

"Then why not write 'near'?"

"Because the end of the world is nigh. Repent."

But the end of the world wasn't nigh. The world was too big, and it had nothing to do with humans, and it could never end. The poor guy just wanted the world to end so his death would coincide with the death of all things. But it never worked out that way. His death would be just as meaningless as everyone else's. But in his religion-encrusted brain Jesus was making a trip around the universe like a comet—Jesus on the comeback trail.

I patted him on the board, and said, "I hope you're right, man. I hope you're right."

I didn't own a watch, but I arrived on time. It had to mean something. But I hadn't set a time to meet Libby, what was I thinking? I locked my bike to a stop sign and went into Pat O'Brien's.

Healthy, sexy, gorgeous Libby was wiping down an old scratched wooden table.

"Hi!" I said, "I'm Nick!"

She said, "Hi," without any enthusiasm. "My name's Susan."

"Susan?"

"Right."

"You're not...Libby?"

A woman came out through the swinging kitchen door. She had long brown hair, her ears stuck out, she didn't have hips, she didn't have breasts. She was as plain-looking as my days were long.

"I've heard so much about you!" she said.

"Yeah?"

"You're my sister's boyfriend's best friend, so you're my friend too!"

I couldn't talk. I needed to turn around and get the hell out of there. I felt so disgusted and embarrassed.

"You want a Guinness?"

"No."

"It's on the house."

"I don't think so."

"What do you want?"

"How about a sparkling water."

She poured a sparkling water from the bar spout. I knew it'd taste flat, but I didn't care, I wasn't going to drink it. I was like a stone standing there that didn't want to be where it was, but, being a stone, it couldn't move. I looked down at my shoes.

After a while Libby said she had to get back to work, she thought her boss might be watching, but Sunday was her day off, and she was thinking about going to the beach in Biloxi, did I want to come along?

I didn't know how to swim, and how do you lay around on a beach all day with someone you don't know, and you don't think you want to get to know? And how do you make plans two days in advance when you won't know how you'll be feeling two days later?

Then again, I'd never been to Biloxi. And I'd never been to the Gulf of Mexico, or even seen an ocean.

"Okay," I said.

I turned to look back at the lovely red-haired Susan who was serving, as if in slow motion, a lucky single man my age. I thought of Darla's angry boyfriend, Eric, the dope dealer. I hoped he'd finally come down off his crack-head high and visit me soon. I just hoped he could shoot straight, and that a bullet, after passing through a closed door could enter a heart sufficiently.

Square Face

The rent was eight days late and my legs were shaking as I waited for her to drag her body to the door. She wore a white nurse's uniform, which surprised me, with gray cigarette ash sprinkled on her ample breast. Her little dog yapped at her side. She kept one hand on the doorknob.

"I'm not gonna pay the rent."

I was prepared for rage, anger, screaming, maybe even spitting and kicking, but she acted like I'd come over for a cup of sugar or a bag of nails. She just worked there. She wasn't the landlord, she didn't care.

"I'm leaving in two days."

I lay on the cool tin balcony, calming down. I was stealing ten days of rent from a landlord I'd never met. He was a bad guy. He had a square jaw and lots of properties.

Fifty Harley-Davidson motorcycles farted up to the stop light down the street and revved their engines.

"Look at me, I'm a fucking rumbling machine!"

"Look at me, my handle bars extend so far I can hardly reach them!"

"Look at me, I'm a little boy all growed up!"

Burly men with gray scraggly beards and women riding behind them with long straight hair wrapped in bandanas.

"Rev, rev, rev!"

"Rev, rev, rev!"

But what if Harleys were driven by black men predominantly? What if black men had made them popular in the first place? What if they were known as "The Black Man's Chopper?" Would Harley's even be legal now? Or would they have been regulated from the start? The noise which interrupts thoughts for miles around, and for minutes at a time, would never have been permitted. Legislators would have nipped that fucking black offense in the bud.

Libby—the feminine "y" ending implied lovely, sweet, and sexy. So did Sandy, Debby, Becky, Cathy, Amy, Betsy, Nancy. Tens of thousands of girls' names—all lovely, sweet and sexy. *Words*—why did I ever think they could be trusted?

I biked Uptown for coffee. I took a walk in Audubon Park. I ate lunch in a grocery store. I took a nap in a different park. I biked to a ferry and rode it all the way to a library in Algiers Point. What was the point? I had nothing better to do than nothing. I went to the Nix Library in Uptown. It was old, small, clean, and un-air-conditioned brick. Slow, twirling ceiling fans, and screen windows that let in bird chirps. I didn't want to hang around for hours. I didn't want to read a book. Life was too long. Books were useless, because none had been written for *me*.

I checked a bulletin board. I saw that Octavia Books was hosting another reading. I didn't write down the information because I didn't want to go.

I hated New Orleans.

I'd plumbed its depths.

I was like an airplane hovering over a landing strip for a couple of days, or a man walking to his car with his keys in his hand.

Milwaukee was calling me home, I had no idea why. Nothing was there for me. Nothing at all.

I counted my money.

My savings were low.

I put off eating for the whole day.

Eventually I went for a bike ride.

I followed a sign for "Garage Sale," block after block. I didn't want to buy anything. I didn't need anything. On a long table, with a hundred other items of junk, was a gun. A gun for sale at a garage sale. A little box of bullets lay beside it. A little gray-bearded white man was selling an old gun. It looked homemade, like a jar of jam. Was there such a thing as a homemade gun? The old man moved slowly toward me, his body listed to the right.

"Can you sell a gun at a garage sale?" I said.

"Sure you can. There it is, can't you see it?"

"But it's not legal, is it?"

"What you gonna do? Buy the damn gun or don't."

I could be armed. Racist Tony, or insane Eric, might come packing. Or it could be used on me. I breathed choppy breaths. Could .22 bullets even break through a skull?

"How much?"

"Twenty."

The same price as the girl!

At night I stayed in and watched TV for hours. A woman whose daughter had been hit and killed by a stray bullet in The Lower Ninth Ward was screaming "Get the f**k out of here!" at a white TV newswoman and the padded microphone that was pushed in her face. I changed the channel.

Pete Seeger was singing in a park alongside the Hudson River while an attractive young white woman far in the background was putting blue jeans on over her bathing suit. Pete changed the lyrics.

> It wasn't your land
> Until you stole it
> For some beads
> You got Manhattan Island

I found an NBA playoff game, a matchup between the Detroit Pistons and The Boston Celtics. I had no interest. I hadn't followed the NBA for years. The outcome, the drama, the high stakes made no difference to me. I watched anyway, every second, for two hours. During the commercials I paced. Then I stared at the screen again and let time get salted away.

When I turned the TV off I felt guilty, like I'd been with another prostitute.

I brushed my teeth and looked at myself in the mirror. Who was that ugly guy? I didn't like him one bit. I sat in the dark and stared at the dark. I went to bed, though I wasn't tired.

The next night I couldn't stay in. I tip-toed my bike carefully down the stairs to avoid Julie and Nick. I rode Uptown in a downpour that would have rotted anybody's shoes. Made it to The Maple Leaf on Oak Street.

A dive, wooden floor, friendly, no cover, a live band, people dancing the Cajun Two Step. Accordion, fiddle, guitar, triangle, tall skinny white guy singing. It reminded me of what life must've been like before it got fucked up, back when communities existed, back when people fell in love while dancing inside a country form.

An old woman, my mother's age, asked me to dance. I liked dancing. Dancing was fun. She moved nimbly, and even led. Then I took a seat on the bench that ringed both sides of the dance floor and nursed a beer, the way my mother had taught me.

The guy who'd sold me my bike was there. And again he was holding a bottle in his left hand, and his left leg was jiggling. His whole body seemed left-handed. He gazed at the good people dancing, and every once in a while he took a sip of beer, at about the same time I sipped. It was horrible. His long curly blond locks and square face.

On the ride home a man in a pickup truck with Louisiana license plates passed me, and I had to pull over to weep, because he was going home and I wasn't.

My plan was to get up in the middle of the night and call Libby and leave a message on her answering machine that said I couldn't make it for whatever fake reason, like I'd been hired to work on a fishing boat, or suddenly I'd caught a bad cold.

Then I decided I wanted to go. A beach in Biloxi sounded interesting. I needed interesting. I rolled over onto my stomach and fell asleep.

I woke up, and didn't want to go. I put my clothes on and grabbed a quarter from the pile, took my clothes off again. "Go to the beach, damn it!"

I woke up and didn't want to go.

I fell asleep.

This went on for hours.

Last Convertible to Biloxi

At Curley's for breakfast. (Just coffee, please.) I saw a hip young white woman poking neat fork holes in her buckwheat pancakes before spreading syrup on them. She made a row of holes one way, then a row of holes the other way. Very neat, schooled, and efficient—while her rooster-headed toddler, dressed in blue mutton-eating clothes, steered the table like he was the captain of a tugboat.

An omen?

I zigzagged north and east, up to Libby's house on Palmyra Street. I'd never been up that way. I walked up and down the block to see what it was like. A middle-aged black man, standing in his front door, glared at me. I glared back, equally untrusting. I asked him, under my breath, "Do you *own* this block?" It so happened that he lived right next door to Libby. I lowered my eyes and opened her gate. Two raised beds in front of the house. Peppers, squash, beans and sunflowers. A flowering plant, maybe a camellia or a rhododendron, six feet tall. Between the gate and the front steps, a black garbage bin stuffed with yard waste that I had to move to get past. Cracks in the cement steps overgrown with weeds. A potted plant in the way. Some kind of red flower that I had to step around.

I'd seen lots of shotgun houses, but I'd never been in one. Hers was about ten feet wide, with a fresh coat of light-green paint. A tiny porch swing in front of the window faced the street. Lace curtains were drawn away from the center, like an elderly lady lived there.

Libby opened the door just before I could knock. She saw my bike locked in front and told me to bring it in. I leaned it against a bookshelf in the tiny, clean living room. She showed me around, through one bedroom to get to another bedroom, and then another. The air was shady and smelled nice. She had two roommates she said.

I asked her what neighborhood we were in, and she said Bayou St. John. She asked me if I wanted a cup of herbal tea. I said sure. She said she'd packed a picnic lunch for us. I was quiet. I was worried I wasn't going to have enough to say later, so I was saving up. Libby didn't seem to mind. When she had something to say she said it. When she talked, she talked quietly and slowly, in a tone that fit an early morning rendezvous with someone she didn't know.

Her skin was tan, and we were going to the beach. But her hair was thin and her ears stuck out, and her eyes were too far apart and her breasts were indefinable. She had lips, teeth, and a forehead—and her nose seemed to be in the right place.

"Nice day for a picnic," she said.

"I think so."

I felt the way old people might feel after their youths are spent. The way they can sit for hours in front of a TV set and stare, or how they can rock back and forth on a front porch all afternoon without needing to think or move.

She asked me if I was hungry, and I said no. But I was kind of hungry. Just a little bite of toast would have been the thing. All I had to say was, "I wouldn't mind a little piece of toast," but I didn't feel relaxed. She didn't seem upset though. She seemed to accept my shyness.

She said she and her housemates were thinking of buying a TV.

I said, "No, don't do it!"

"Why not? I like TVs, they're useful. You just have to know how to turn them off."

"Well."

She drove a red VW Bug. I was surprised by how sharp, new, and expensive it looked. It was the new design, with the plastic flower sticking up for everyone to know it was a girl's car. It had a cream-colored convertible top. "Oh, I see you took out the flower."

"I cut it out the first day."

"It sure is a nice car."

"I worked seven years as a preschool teacher so I thought, 'I'm going to buy a car I like!'"

I couldn't disagree.

She pushed a button and the roof rolled down, and we flipped our visors down at the same time. We grinned.

She said, "It'll take an hour and a half, give or take a minute."

We hit the freeway.

She was driving, so I thought I should steer the conversation.

"What sign are you?"

"Sagittarius. Are you into astrology?"

"Not really."

A preschool teacher, hmm. The lowest of the low. Dumbing it down for kids all day. Buying materials out of her own pocket. A teacher's lounge full of small-minded creeps.

She slid a CD into the player—Kristin Hersh's *Hips and Makers*—and I about lost it. The songs all sounded alike, and her voice was flat and shrill.

"Take it out! Take it out!" I shouted.

She was going to, but I stopped her.

"Just kidding," I said.

I wasn't kidding.

Before a warehouse party in the Flagship neighborhood, I'd talked Colette and two of her friends into driving out to "Mistake Lake" to lose some money playing blackjack, but they were only living for the warehouse party. Then, after the ding-ding-ding of the casino and the long drive back I said I wanted to eat at a Chinese restaurant that Colette hated, but I'd never eaten there, and I wanted to judge it for myself. Colette crossed her arms, and kept them crossed for the rest of the ride home—all while Kristin Hersh's *Hips and Makers* played —from Milwaukee to Mistake Lake and back that awful sound drilled itself into me, deeper and deeper, and became forever associated with one fucked up day.

Warm Louisiana wind blew into our faces. I ran my fingers through my hair—still, sadly, too short to worry. I tried to smile, but couldn't. I stuck my elbow out the window like an expert convertible rider. Libby laughed. I asked her what was so funny.

"Everything! It's a beautiful day!"

The top was down, so it was hard to talk. That was good. I could make it all the way to Biloxi in one piece. But how do you sit on a beach all day? What is expected of a person with only sun, sky, hot sand, and a stranger? My first voyage out of New Orleans.

Libby pushed a button and the roof rolled up. She told me she was involved in a ménage a trois. I didn't bat an eyelash. I was totally liberal when it came to other people's complicated sex lives. I questioned her like a reporter.

"What's that like?"

"Well, it started out wonderful, but now it's, complicated. Love and pain, are like, the same?"

"How did it start?"

"We were friends, Nomi and I. She started dating Jeff, then things got, well, I'm not sure how but, Jeff is kind of, he holds back a lot, you know? So a rift is growing and, I don't know what to do."

I stopped being a reporter when her eyes began to glisten, then a big tear rolled down her cheek.

"It has to end. I just don't know how."

I pursed my lips.

Knowing that Libby was in a relationship, with not one but two people, helped me to relax. I knew she had no designs on me. Not that I'd thought she did, but then I knew. I breathed better.

I liked how she'd shared, without being asked, in all frankness, a huge part of her private life. She'd gotten right down to it. She was brave, this Libby person, whoever she was—all while Kristin Hersh warbled crisp, sharp and ugly on the VW Bug's fine stereo system.

We talked about the one thing we had in common, her sister. She said they grew up in North Carolina, moved to Tennessee, and had always lived in the country. Their mom was a hippy, their dad an accountant. They'd gone around in the nude a lot when they were little, and still did often when they went home. They had an older brother who'd been killed in a car accident when he was sixteen—and her sister was fifteen, and Libby was nine. Their dad couldn't take it, and he left them and moved to Kentucky where he became a motorcycle mechanic. She said her sister took on their brother's personality after that. It was uncanny how she kind of became him. Before that she'd been the brain in the family, the one who got A's without trying, and she always came straight home from school, etc., and never went out on weekends.

"Is that the same girl I know?" I said.

"I know! She changed so much. How is she these days, by the way?"

"I haven't seen her in, in a month and a half."

I had no reason to hold back information, but I hesitated to tell Libby that her sister told crazy stories about sucking men off in bathroom stalls and how she "left them hanging." And she'd had sex with several of my friends, even twice with me, so when she'd become my best friend's girlfriend I didn't think it'd last a week, but then it had, so now who knew anything? And, her breasts were too big and sloshy for me—that was something I'd never tell anyone.

We pulled into a parking lot next to a long stretch of white sandy beach, just as *Hips and Makers* was ending. I'd fallen in love with Kristen Hersh!

The hypnotic rhythm of her guitar and her raw vocals struck me as soaring and gutsy. Her guitar strumming built up, came down, but never came all the way down. Her voice was strong, clear, strange and unpretentious. Her whole sound left traces of beauty splashed all over me.

> I could get a piece of meat
> From a barren tree
> Nothing ever spoiled on me

Libby carried the beach blanket and towels, and suntan lotion and sunscreen, and beach chairs, and a book for herself, and a half dozen books for me to choose from in a wicker basket—while I carried the cooler and wondered if she was gay.

She rubbed sunscreen on her arms and face and legs. She didn't take off her shirt or shorts. I took off my shirt. She put on a straw hat and sunglasses. I squinted and she looked for a second like Lolita. She offered me her straw hat. I gallantly accepted. It was tiny and sat on the tip of my head.

Were we ready?

She leaned back, adjusted the book's position in relation to her lap and the angle of the sun. I could see the cover, *Annie John*. I didn't respect Jamaica Kincaid.

But I'd been raised in a house with a black bible, a green dictionary, and a large cardboard box full of comic books left to us by an aunt. I felt so far behind, sometimes, that I didn't even want to catch up.

I looked through her wicker basket of goodies, and found another book, *The Stranger*, by Camus. Funny thing, I couldn't remember a thing about it. Strange to have read a book, and loved it, and then totally not know anything about it. I looked at the cover: four sexless humans in whiteface wearing three-foot tall striped hats.

I squinted at the ocean. Oil rigs in the distance. Far away, or close, depending. I counted —one, two, three, four, five oil rigs interrupting the horizon of baked sky and flat ocean receding.

I couldn't concentrate. The sun was too bright. But then I'd never been very good at concentrating. I was good at losing track, and waking up somewhere else. I put Camus down. I lifted him up. I held him. The sand on the beach was too white. I'd never seen sand so white.

I looked at the oil rigs. I looked at the sun. I looked at my legs. I looked at Libby and wanted to talk, but I knew she was talking—or rather, listening to *Annie John*—that disposable, nothing of a book.

I wriggled in my lawn chair. I tried to settle in. Libby was a good role model. I had hope. I was on a beach. I was kind of already doing it. I felt hungry.

Did I dare take something from the cooler without asking? Did I dare nibble grapes and cheese without asking first if she wanted any? I asked Libby if she wanted any grapes and cheese. "No thanks. Go ahead though." So I took some for myself. They were sweet and cold. I told her I was going for a walk. She said okay. I liked her.

I walked on the beach. Hot sand scorched my toes. I dropped Libby's hat on the sand and ran into the water, warm and clear. I waded in up to my throat. If only I knew how to swim. Libby, of course, knew how to swim. Everybody knew how to swim but me. I put my head underwater and held my breath. The saltiness lifted me up. I floated on my back. The glare of the sun on my eyes was sharp. I felt wobbly and dizzy walking back to shore. My shoulders had already begun to burn. Why hadn't I called

Libby sooner? Why had I waited until the very end of my time to do it?

I picked up her hat and put it back on the tip of my head. I walked along the beach to a fake Tiki lounge. I sat under a blue tarp next to some kids who were drinking margaritas out of clear plastic cups. They didn't seem to be enjoying themselves. They seemed like college roommates who hadn't been able to break up yet.

I said to the bartender, "Tonic water, please." I didn't know it'd taste so awful. I didn't know tonic existed only for mixed drinks—gin and *tonic*, never *tonic* by itself. I looked at the label—what was quinine?

The sad kids burst out laughing. Did I look funny wearing Libby's tiny straw hat on the top of my head? I tipped my head back and pushed the hat forward onto my nose, and looked through the meshed brim at them. It was like looking through a haystack. I laughed too.

Libby was sleeping on her stomach when I got back, her head turned away. I liked her. I sat down on my beach chair and reached over for *Annie John* which was sitting face-down on the blanket.

Annie John is a haunting and provocative story of a young girl growing up on the island of Antigua. A classic coming-of-age story in the tradition of *The Catcher in the Rye* and *A Portrait of the Artist as a Young Man*, Kincaid's novel focuses on a universal, tragic, and often comic theme: the loss of childhood. Annie's voice—urgent, demanding to be heard—is one that will not soon be forgotten by readers.

When I first met Colette she was reading Amy Hempel, and I couldn't stand her either. The style was too exact and false. But Colette loved Amy Hempel—like a lot of other would-be John Updikes and Raymond Carvers did. But I couldn't even begin to read her.

Libby rolled over and beamed. I was on page twenty-six. What a great book! Simple, direct, pure narration. She asked me if I wanted to go for a walk. There was a cemetery across the highway she wanted to show me.

We stood up, brushed sand off, and took two bottles of water out of the cooler. We waited for traffic to open up, then ran across the highway. We walked under an ivy arch, with an iron sign above it that read Old French Cemetery. Graves, tall shade trees, people strolling—and a mausoleum that blew us away.

A wealthy person had recreated a minia-ture interior of his mansion, remade in marble, with furniture, appliances even (toasters and lamps and bookshelves and books and rugs), all remade in marble, in one-tenth scale or something. Like something Ted Turner might do. We peered through the bedroom window, past the fixed, forever frozen-in-the-breeze marble curtains. I expected to see him lying on the bed, taking a nap with his hat beside him, but the bed was empty. Libby thought he might be in the living room sitting on the couch, so we ran around to look. "Nobody home!" said Libby. It was so funny I fell down on the grass laughing. Mortal people and the pride they have.

I told Libby it'd be fun to picket a funeral, to hold up picket signs that read, "Down with Coffins!" She agreed it was a funny idea, and she'd picket with me. I asked her if she'd picket her own mother's funeral, and she said she wouldn't, that'd be too much, but she'd picket *my* mother's funeral. Nice touch.

We sat under the oldest living shade tree in Mississippi. I took off my hat. She took off her sunglasses. She grinned, but not at me. I didn't mind. Thirty yards away—I can't measure these things—a young woman with green strands in her blond hair was sitting on a park bench beside an Indian or Pakistani young man. She was wearing an aquamarine hearing aid that stood out from her ear on purpose like a cool pair of eyeglasses. She handed him a drawing she'd been making on her artist's pad. He examined it, nodded, and handed it back. Her deafness as a child had affected her speech, so she was often quiet, and the young man, out of love and respect, was quiet too. After awhile, the young Indian or Pakistani man said goodbye and walked away, straight toward us. We pretended to be talking. When he was past, we gazed back at her. She was putting her art things away. Then she leaned forward and began sketching something with her left hand. Her blond hair with green streaks fell into her face. Her pink, long-sleeved men's cotton shirt. Her aqua marine hearing aid. So beautiful.

It was the first time in my life that I'd been so quiet, and thoughtful, and observant alongside another person.

We had to wait at the edge of the highway for a long string of cars to pass, then we made a run for it. We ran all the way back to our spot on the beach. The sun was even more intense. I wanted to lead us into something new. I ran into the water. Libby followed. We were up to our throats when I told her the most important dream I'd ever had.

I was in a bookstore. I went to the Fiction section. I went to the first three letters of my last name: *Sch*...and there on the shelf was a book I'd written...but its author was Kilmore Dog.

"Kill more dog?"

"I know! I don't get it either. I mean, what *is* a dog? And what part of a dog am I supposed to *kill* in order to be published?

"I had that dream three years ago when I thought I wanted to be a writer. That's why I started driving cab. What do you think it means, Libby?"

She was crying.

"I think you need to do something very serious with your life yet to understand this dream."

We packed and drove out of the parking lot silently. As we turned left onto the highway, *Hips and Makers* started playing at the beginning as if on cue. Brilliant. Libby drove fast— was she in a hurry to get rid of me?

I didn't tell her that I'd read the whole first page of Kilmore Dog's novel, and it was brilliant, but when I'd tried to bring back it up—Orpheus-like—it disappeared. It was so disappointing that I'd written a great book without my own knowledge, and I couldn't have it.

That was one reason why I loved to sleep so much—because in sleep at least there was the chance to meet the writer, or person, I could have, or should have been—but somehow I'd taken the wrong path.

Libby pressed the button that put the top down, and started talking about the ménage a trois again, like being in the car with the top down triggered it.

"Jeff can be very charismatic. He made a recording once of his voice; he channeled a trembling old black man, and told rambling funny family stories from way back on the cotton plantation; he erased himself completely and became that old black man. We loved it, and begged him to study acting, but Jeff doesn't study anything, he wants to invent himself without any help from anybody at any time. And anyway, he was already on to the next thing.

"He can be awful too. He does a lot of drugs, and when he's high he doesn't have any fear, or shame—or compassion either. I've gotten used to it, kind of, but I mean, I know how mercurial he can be, and how violent too—and how easily broken!

"He was high once, on mushrooms, and he lay down in the middle of a street, because he truly believes death is a lie society tells its young ones to control them...but at the same time he just wanted to die because life can be so overwhelming!

"But he'd never admit that. Of course not. When I try to bring up anything like that—like the contradictions in whatever he's doing—he gets defensive. I mean, he can get downright angry. Because he hates limits so much! He hates it when anyone even talks about limits... but he hates kindness too, and patience, and loyalty—all the things I admire so much!

"Once, when he was high on Ecstasy and cocaine, with Nomi, before I knew either of them, he asked her to reenact a rape scene. He'd become convinced that, in a former life, he'd raped a girl, and to overcome it he had to exorcize it—and Nomi went along with it because she believed in him completely. Even when he became violent, with real pushing and shoving, and real hitting—he gave her a black eye and ripped up her bed sheets—Nomi never once thought that *Jeff* was doing those things."

Dusk. Heavy, stodgy freeway traffic. Quiet between us. A line of cars heading back into New Orleans on a quiet Sunday night. Big billboards loomed, one after another. I read them silently.

Dave's Hot 'n Juicy Cheeseburgers.
'Here's the Beef, Wendy's!'

A hamburger dressed up like a model, air-brushed pickles and onions, ketchup dripping down her naked meat like semen. It wasn't hunger of the stomach they were aiming at, it was that everyone was horny and they knew it. Top secret, shh.

Calvin Klein.
"Perfect Fit."

A black and white photo of a woman, thin and gorgeous, billowy 60s-style hair, reclining in just black panties, a black bra, and black stiletto shoes, her legs three-quarters spread.

The Friendship House Restaurant.
'Howdy Folks!'

Three crawfish and a crab, all wearing chef's hats, waving to us, inviting us come on in and eat them.

Skimming through the warm darkness on the long bridge over Lake Pontchartrain—like the dream I used to have as a kid, of driving on a long bridge over an enormous body of water, on and on and on—of course the bridge collapsed, and I woke up terrified.

Other people knew how to string together a whole lifetime of days like this, but I couldn't. I was renting my body like an apartment building. I wanted to ask Libby how she did it, but I didn't want her to know me. Like the song said, "A short time here, a long time gone"—all while Kristin Hersh sang.

> I married a boxer to keep me from fighting
> I married a brewer to keep me from drinking
> We have a good time, they keep me dancing

Libby asked me if I wanted to have dinner at her house. She was going to throw together a Greek salad and something else. I was disappointed. I wanted to eat at a nice restaurant. I never got to eat out in nice places because I was alone so much. Also, being in public, and eavesdropping, would've been more fun and less intimacy-inducing.

Besides, we'd already had a full day. I was content with what we'd already accomplished. I didn't want to press my luck any further. I thought about saying no.

Colette hated when I eavesdropped. She said it was rude to listen to other people's conversations. I said the social contract allows for eavesdropping. In fact, it *encourages* eavesdropping! She said well, then, if you prefer listening to strangers so much, then it shows there's a serious flaw in our relationship, and maybe we should just be strangers.

The Great American Handshake

I washed my face, hands and underarms. Water dripped on the floor and I wiped it up carefully with toilet paper. I went into Libby's kitchen. She was mixing salad in a wooden bowl with huge wooden tongs. I asked her if there was anything I could do to help, and she said I should go into the living room and relax, lie down on the couch if I wanted to. I lay down and shut my eyes.

Colette said, "I want to have a child."

I said, "No, you want to *be* a child."

"You don't understand. I want to hold a child, under my wing."

"You really want to have a child—with me?"

I believed her, for one second.

Libby's cell phone rang...

Once Colette made up her mind that I wasn't the one she started to treat me badly. It was like she'd flipped a switch and became mean and not beautiful.

Or, by pushing me away was she daring me to stay?

I didn't ask.

I wasn't straight-shooting enough to even think of asking.

Libby said, "Jeff and Nomi were at a movie. They're on their way home. They want to meet you too!"

I opened my eyes.

Purple and deep green curtains. A worn out, but warm oriental rug in the center of a gray-painted wooden floor. Three walls lined with homemade bookshelves, a half-dead cactus, found furniture, walls painted pale orange and blue. What a lovely, lived-in home.

My bike was resting, as it had been all day, up against a row of books, like it lived there.

I heard voices so I sat up. I couldn't do anything about what was going to happen. I would try to impress them by talking too much. I told myself to shut up and listen.

Jeff came into the living room. He was a black man. He had short hair. His eyelids were sad. He had a weird, thick mustache. He wore weird, square silver studs in his earlobes. His body was thick. He was like a bull. He came in close and gave me a bear hug.

"Fuck the great American handshake!" he said.

A gentle bull.

Nomi kissed me on both cheeks. She had freckles on her nose and cheeks. Her skin was very white, her lips pink. No lipstick. She smiled. Her teeth were crooked and lovely, and I thanked her parents for not getting them fixed when she was little. So feminine, so natural.

Not what I'd expected.

What had I expected? How could I have pictured them, when they hadn't even been described to me? I looked at Jeff—he was taking me in.

"Now that we've all met!" said Libby.

I flashed on us as a foursome. If three, then why not four? Who writes the codes? Who makes the rules for us to obey?

"Preposterous," I said.

They looked at me.

"*Pre...posterior...ous*'—it means 'Put your ass in front!'"

They laughed.

They liked me?

Jeff said he was starving, and Nomi stuck her belly out and drew a circle around it, and pointed to it. I scratched my scalp.

In the kitchen we scooped plates full of Greek Salad and angel hair pasta topped with tomato sauce "made fresh from tomatoes, garlic, onions, basil, and oregano from the garden."

Their garden.

We sat down in the living room, plates balancing on our laps. There wasn't a dining room table, but there were three antique reading lamps—I liked their priorities.

The sweet smell of oregano, garlic, and tomato somehow matched the orange and blue walls, the purple and green curtains.

Jeff ate like a ten year-old boy, red sauce dribbling down his chin. It looked like Nomi hadn't washed her hair in a week. Libby's thin hair was tucked behind her ears, which made them stick out even more.

They seemed comfortable together, like normal roommates. If Libby hadn't told me, I would never have guessed. They didn't touch, or look at each other in telling ways.

I was leaving.

I'd waited until the very end to call Libby, and now I was leaving.

Would they like me less if I told them I was a ghost just passing through?

Nomi asked me if I did drugs. Was she going to break out the stuff?

I said, "I used to, about ten years ago."

"Why did you stop?"

"My mind opened up like a flower and... slammed shut like a valve?"

They laughed.

It was true—from velvety petal to metal valve, that was me.

Jeff clapped his hands. "I'm going to find the meaning of life through drugs! I really am. It probably sounds absurd but..."

"No, not absurd," I said.

He reached over like he was going to put an Ecstasy pill on my knee, and Libby blushed. Nomi noticed, too, that she was sunburned, and she went to the bathroom and came back out with a bottle of Aloe Vera.

She rubbed some on Libby's sunburned face and shoulders, then made a motion with the bottle toward me. I undid the top three buttons of my shirt and slid it off my shoulders and closed my eyes.

We sat in the small garden area behind the house in the dark, drinking iced peach tea. I felt conservative compared to them. I wanted to know what was coming next. Then I swelled with love ten times my body size. Anything I'd thought I understood about their ménage a trois, or any ménage a trois, had to be wrong. I admired them for what they were attempting. And I sensed that Jeff's personality was so strong it included negative qualities normal people wouldn't allow in, but to Jeff they just had to be. He lived completely and without compromise, so others had to react, or else. He wasn't the kind of person you can walk away from easily, and then feel okay about yourself afterward. The rape scene, I kept thinking about the rape scene.

I looked at Libby. She looked at me. I wanted to dive in and vomit up my present life, but I was afraid I couldn't do it. In the cricket and cicada-loud night and my sad-as-hell leaving.

Colette started calling me Uncle Nick at one point. I told her to cut it out, that it hurt. She said I didn't know how to take a joke; if I knew how to take a joke, I'd laugh when she called me Uncle Nick, and then she wouldn't call me Uncle Nick anymore.

That was about the time she told me I didn't have a soul, which was meant to really hurt me, so I laughed. But that only made her mad for some reason.

Jeff plugged in the Christmas lights—the old-fashioned, big bulb kind—and the big tree in the back yard lit up in colors. While Nomi rolled a cigarette.

I wondered if she cut her own hair, or if Libby cut it. Her bones were fine, her face too. Nomi was...*gnomey*?

If I only had a soul.

What she was smoking wasn't tobacco.

"It's my own mix," and she ticked off the ingredients. "Coltsfoot, sage, marshmallow leaf, mullein, lavender, a whole bunch of other things, and a little bit of tobacco. Want some?" She tossed me the bag. I felt around inside.

"What's the furry stuff?"

"That's mullein."

She was the most beautiful person in the backyard. I had to look away. More beautiful than Libby? More beautiful than Jeff? More beautiful than...me? I spilled some of it on my lap, then the paper broke.

"Here," she said, "Let me do it."

Dirty blond hair hung down and covered her face. If I had a face like that I'd draw attention away from it too.

"Nomi is an unusual name," I said.

They laughed—had they heard it so many times before?

"My real name's Naomi, but I pronounce it Nomi."

"No *me*!" said Jeff—"very Buddhist."

"Jeff!" said Libby, "What movie did you see?"

"Well, it was a sad and slow movie that we didn't even know we liked until we got so involved in the family that it was like we were in their home, so when the main character, a teenage girl, started to weep, we started to weep too."

"An amazing film!" said Nomi. "You have to see it. It'll be showing for another week, I think."

Jeff looked at the ground like other people look at the sky, and said, "Thank you, great Indian director whose name I can't remember, for this movie you have given us tonight."

It was like I was there, but wasn't. I sat in the colorful darkness, a happy mosquito. I imagined them in bed together. I saw them wrestling around. Jeff lit a cigar.

Jeff, of all people, smoking cigars? The stench and bullying posture of cigars? *After* lighting it he asked me if I minded. I tried to put this in line with what I'd been told, or what I thought I knew about him.

I don't know why it was time to go, but it was. I stood up and said, "It's time to go"—just as Jeff was lighting a joint.

Libby and Nomi saw me out. We stood in the doorway. Nomi said she worked at The Hippie Gypsy on Canal Street, I should drop by any time. Libby said she'd had a wonderful day, and we should do it again sometime. "Wait a second," she said, and went back in the house, and came out with a small paper sack. "Clementine oranges, for you, from us, to take home!"

Home—wherever that was.

The wooden screen door shut, then I was on the other side. The day was back there, a memory already. A memory just starting out.

The same middle-aged black man as before, the one who lived next door to them, was standing on his front steps with his elbows stuck out. Why did he hate me? What had I done to him? Or did he hate Jeff, a fellow black man, because he lived with two white women? Did he know the three of them were lovers? Or was he homophobic? Or was he jealous? Or was his life pathetic, and he wished he was Jeff—a young, powerful, and virile man who lived with two white women?

I said as kindly as I could to him, "Have a nice evening."

He blasted a shaft of hatred into me.

Rover, Come Back

A boy was selling small pieces of white tape but I didn't want to buy any. Then I reached for the tape and the boy handed some to me. I put pieces of it over the sore in my mouth, where a loose piece of skin had pulled away from the gum.

There was a metal ring around my neck. I assumed there was a correlation between the ring and my mouth. If my mouth healed the ring would go away. The ring was like a dog collar, or slave collar, loose enough to not quite choke me. I knew the ring around my neck was never coming off. I knew I had to wear it forever—as an identification or tracking collar. For some strange reason I felt gratitude. A feeling of complete trust—like a tamed wild animal.

My flight was at 11:30 that night. The red-eye. I intended to ship my bike home, but then decided I'd go to the bike shop and see if I could sell it back. The guy I'd bought it from wasn't there. I got one-fourth of what I'd paid for it. I walked out feeling okay. I walked all the way up to PJs, in fact. A hot windy day.

I waited for a newspaper to be abandoned, then picked it up. The wind made reading hard. I'd be reading a paragraph, then the wind would flip the page. I hated the wind. Then I thought of Libby and Nomi and Jeff, and how they probably loved the wind, or at least they would've been happy to work with it, and not scold it.

The leaves on the tall maple tree in the backyard of PJ's blew backward so I could see their silver underbellies. I wondered if the wind was strengthening the trunk of the tree. And did I have a trunk that was being strengthened too, by a strong wind? Did I have roots that went down deep into the earth and grabbed hold?

A homeless old man on the sidewalk was bent over weeping. I pitied him, and went over to help him, but when I got there he was talking to himself and laughing.

I walked down Audubon Boulevard which was under construction. Jackhammers and men in white helmets and vests working day and night to make sense of being on this strange planet.

I walked without meaning to, all the way up to Bayou St. John. I thought, "Might as well drop in. Walk up to their door and knock. Be in their living room. Take advantage of the coincidence."

My last day in New Orleans.

Finn McCool's was right around the corner from Libby's house, I didn't know that.

It was dark and empty. I ordered a beer and went to the backyard. It was packed with boys and girls in their mid-twenties, dressed in kickball uniforms, eye-black on their cheeks.

Julie had been talking right there. That was where she'd told me about the pornographic hermit neighbor. I looked up. The moon was in the blue sky like a pale curved bone.

I pulled a Clementine orange out of my shoulder bag and ate it, and was glad Colette had gone and done something stupid like getting engaged to her x-boyfriend. She wasn't the one. We'd never gone deep, and never would have. She'd run away from me as much as she'd run to him. She—who at one time had claimed marriage was an outmoded institution in which two people agreed, irrationally, to wall themselves off to have offspring, and buy a split-level house in the suburbs, and lose their friends—was now getting married, and soon, no doubt, she'd conceive a child, and in a year or two they'd buy a house, and a few years later they'd buy a bigger one, all for their expanding dreams to die in.

She had to live with that, I didn't. I only had to accept that even a good person can say one thing and do the opposite.

I ran to Libby's house to tell her that Colette was getting married in June. This month. That maybe she was already married. It began to rain. In books about dreams it's said that rain is a symbol of change—so, then, in New Orleans everything was always changing? I ran fast.

I ran right past their house, right past the scowling black man's house, all the way around the block, back to Finn McCool's. I hailed a cab that slammed on its brakes because I was young and white and looked harmless.

Back home on the balcony I counted my money in the kitchen. I stood up, and looked across the street. Racist Tony and a half dozen of his pals were in the front yard listening to loud, thumping rap music. I crouched. I didn't want our two worlds to collide ever again. The air was hot and sticky. Over ninety degrees. No relief. No wind. I went to the corner store to see what I could see.

I decided to walk all the way up to the Maple Street Bookshop, four miles. I wanted to buy a book for the airplane. I went to the Fiction section, as was my habit. I looked for the first three letters of my last name—*Sch*—to see if Kilmore Dog had written any books lately.

I picked up a book called *Black Sexual Politics: African Americans, Gender, and the New Racism*. I leafed through it. Four hundred pages long. I picked up a book called *The Heart of Whiteness: Confronting Race, Racism and White Privilege*. A hundred and twenty-four pages—just right.

I hailed a taxi. I was running out of money. Fuck it. The driver was a white guy about my age. His hair, however, was six months longer than mine, and he was smoking a cigarette, and when I got in he kept on smoking. He had no clue.

He asked me what kind of music I liked. I said, "Oh, I don't know, Kristen Hersh?" He said he was into a German metal band, and he slid a CD in and the music blasted. He shouted over it.

"Yesterday I drove all the way out to my home in Slidell at 2:30 to meet the cable guy! Two hours later, he still hadn't come! I was so pissed off I called the cable company! And they said, 'He called you at 2:13 and you didn't answer!' What a fucking jerk thing to do! I was supposed to meet the cable guy between two and four!"

I said, "But isn't 2:13 between two and four?"

He said everybody was out to get him— corporations, the government, student loan organizations, everybody! He said he'd really, *really* been looking forward to having cable last night.

I didn't know if I should tip him twenty dollars because he was my sad lost twin, or if I should stiff him because he was my sad lost twin. I split the difference, and gave him two bucks over the meter.

I pushed the TV into the hallway, which scratched the floor, but the floor was already scratched. I put the extension cord and ice cube tray on top of the TV and went inside my apartment to write a note.

Nick and Julie,
Thanks for letting me use your stuff,
Nick.

I taped it to the door.

I stood on the balcony one last time and thought of triangles. If A is on top, then B and C are underneath. Say Jeff is A, and Libby and Nomi are B and C.

But it doesn't have to be that way. A triangle can spin! You can blow on a triangle like a pinwheel, and it can spin! Everyone can take a turn on top.

I wanted to tell Libby the good news about triangles, but luckily I didn't have a cell phone, so I had the pleasure of wanting to call her without the burden of actually calling her. She was like a dream already.

I stuffed my backpack full of what I'd come to New Orleans with, and went and knocked on the caretaker lady's door. Her hair was wet and freshly combed back. She invited me in. Her dog was nowhere to be seen. I handed her the key. She asked if I wanted something to drink. I didn't. She'd expected nothing of me all along? I liked her. I might've even gotten to know her.

I said, "I have to be going."

She said, "I wish you the best of luck in all your future endeavors." She touched my hand, which reminded me of my mother who only seemed to want to touch me when I was leaving.

Julie was standing by the mailboxes reading a letter.

"Do people still write letters?"

"Some do, apparently."

"I'm leaving."

"I see that."

I turned sideways to scrape past her with my backpack.

"Have a nice trip."

I wanted to apologize, say something like "It was all a misunderstanding. I don't know myself well enough to have intelligent arguments. I'm sorry."

But I didn't say that.

As I walked away I turned to say goodbye—to Darla.

Darla, who was still upstairs, still lying on the floor after all this time, her face and shirt soaked in sweat and blood, passed out from either being drunk or beaten.

They were through.

It was final.

This was it.

Eric slammed the door shut and leapt down the stairs, hurdling his body. He didn't know where he was going, or what he was going to go to, only that he had to get away from there.

I hadn't thought about Darla for a long time. I hoped she was doing well, wherever she was, whoever she was with.

But I didn't know Darla.

I'd never met her.

All I had was a note stabbed through a nail on a door and three photographs that fell out from under a mattress.

I called Super Shuttle from outside Curley's, then waited. I waited until I thought it wasn't going to come, then it came. We made a stop downtown, then five more stops in different neighborhoods. Everybody was alone. All the single people were leaving New Orleans. Nobody said a word. On the freeway, approaching the airport, planes hovered in line in the sky waiting to land, like big guided bullets.

I strolled from business to business on the main concourse. I wanted to buy something, but there was nothing I wanted. I bought a Snickers bar to make the economy feel better. I put it inside myself. "You should see it all!" said a kid about something.

I had the last Clementine orange in my backpack, and I felt sentimental toward it. I thought I might smuggle it back to Milwaukee, or not eat it at all. I might let it dry and shrink to become a memento—and then nail it to a living room wall I hadn't rented yet.

I ate it. It was just too easy to peel and segment. Too simple not to eat. I went to the men's room to rinse off my hands.

A bleary-eyed college girl, wearing faded bib overalls and a super-over-sized red sombrero, and a couple dozen Mardi Gras beads around her neck, stomped hard and squeaked playfully in her unlaced tennis shoes on the super-polished airport floor. She must have partied pretty hardy the night before.

I drank a cup of coffee that tasted sour. My plane was going to board, but not soon. I couldn't find a clock anywhere. Funny that an airport wouldn't have a clock. I wrote on a napkin, like I was talking to someone, "Something has to give." I was in an airport full of ghosts wandering around between where they'd come from and where they were going.

Why was I flying back to Milwaukee anyway? Nothing and nobody was waiting for me. I'd resist walking to Colette's house for a week, then I'd walk to her house and peek in through the window. No, I'd move back in with my parents first!

Things were going to happen, one after another, for many years to come yet—was I ready for that?

I noticed on an electronic flight board that my flight was delayed in Dallas. I walked up and down the concourse, past shops, security guards, the same shops. I ate a Baby Ruth candy bar. I had a second cup of sour coffee. I was getting angry. I was getting pissed off. I was getting restless. I didn't care if I died in mid-air. I hoped the plane would crash in a corn field in Iowa. I went down to the baggage claim.

A fifty-year-old woman with hair dyed red looked like a cheesy female novelist. She'd bought a copy of her own novel in Pittsburgh at an airport convenience store, then she'd boarded the plane and opened it up in the middle and waited for someone to strike up a conversation. No one did. She asked the woman seated beside her, "Have you ever read this author? I think she's wonderful!" But the woman had never heard of her. Then, when the plane landed in New Orleans, she'd walked to an airport bar and ordered a martini, and opened the book somewhere in middle, and pretended to be reading. The man next to her said, "I don't read garbage like that." But who was he? Just some airport drunk!

My imagination was well-oiled and working fine. But it wasn't enough—and it would never be enough. I had to call Libby—and Nomi, and maybe even Jeff—to tell them about the cheesy female novelist! I had to tell them about Colette, and why I'd come down to New Orleans in the first place. I had tell them about Nick and Julie, and what was wrong with *me*, and why I was leaving New Orleans, and how sorry I was, but I was already holding a ticket in my hand.

I had to calm down.

Libby, Nomi, and Jeff were just three people I'd met. They were like Ellen, the creamy-skinned beauty I'd kissed in the doorway and loved sweetly one night.

People we meet in real life are no different than the people we meet in dreams. Either
way, after they're gone, they become dim and
dimmer memories. And there are always more
people. The world is full of people. People are
no big deal.

Some young people in their twenties huddled
together, hopped up and down. One of them,
holding a bugle, was dressed in a tattered shirt
and pants, and his hair was chopped up, like
he cut it himself, and he stood on his tiptoes
like a little kid, and his shoes had no shoelaces.
He stuck the bugle down his pants, covered the
top part of it with his shirt, and laughed. I saw
that one of his front teeth was missing. How
ugly, how brave.

A girl in her early twenties came stream-
ing off a plane, and he whipped out his bugle
and blasted "Charge!" and the group rushed
her, and they wrapped their arms around her,
and they formed a circle around her, and they
jumped up and down and chanted.

Many people stared, but nobody cared.

I went to a pay phone to call Libby, to tell her
I was leaving. She didn't answer, and I didn't

want to leave a message like that, so I hung up, and went to an airport lounge to have a drink. I said, "I'll have a whiskey sour"—like an adult would.

I focused on the stewardesses, or flight attendants, walking by. They all seemed to walk with very straight backs as they pulled their cute little suitcases on wheels behind them. And their asses swiveled perfectly with each high-heeled runway step they took. I whispered to one of them, long after she'd passed, "You have *jet-black* hair, did anyone ever tell you that?"

Nothing had changed.

It hit me hard.

"Would you like another drink, Sir?"

I didn't care for his tone. It implied I was somebody who commanded respect. I didn't command anything. Besides, the bartender was an actor, and I was tired of actors. I was tired of all the people in the world acting, and getting paid for it, going around acting out their parts.

I waited at Gate B, but instead of waiting I went up to the woman standing behind the gate desk and asked her if the plane had been loaded yet. She checked the computer screen, asked someone, who asked someone, then said, "No Sir, it hasn't been loaded yet."

I asked her if I could take my backpack home with me. She looked on the computer screen, asked someone, who asked someone, then said, "No Sir, your luggage is on a cart and cannot be retrieved now; however, if you would like you may pick it up as early as tomorrow morning."

"Fine, I'll pick it up tomorrow."

The cab driver asked me where I was from, and where I was going, and why didn't I have any luggage. I said I was from New Orleans, and I was going to New Orleans, that was why I didn't have any luggage. He didn't bother me after that. He listened to some kind of African music, and when he dropped me off at the youth hostel I tipped him five bucks for leaving me alone.

I talked to the Siberian guy—Vasily was his name. I hadn't been able to remember it the whole time until I saw his face again. We talked for a long time at the front desk. He wanted to know what I'd been up to.

I had to think.

What had I been up to?

"Not much."

Vasily said a postcard had come for me awhile back. He dug around in the wicker basket full of dead letters and postcards that'd been sent to people who'd left the hostel and would probably never be back. I didn't remember giving Colette my address.

On the front of the postcard was a black and white reproduction of a photo of a pair of leather gloves folded like hands on a table. The caption, below the folded gloves with no hands in them, read: "You are seduced by the sex appeal of the inorganic."

What did it mean? Or rather, what was it *meant* to mean?

On the back she'd written, "I hope you're having fun in New Orleans. All the best, Colette!"

Vasily let me use the desk phone. Nomi answered. We talked a long time. If Jeff had answered, would we have talked for a long time? Nomi said she had to go to work, but I could visit her if I wanted to. We could talk more there.

I went to the bathroom to count my money. I waited a reasonable amount of time in the lobby, then I took the number 11 bus downtown to Canal Street, and found The

Hippie Gypsy easily. A song by Pavement was
blasting on the stereo.

> I want a range life
> If I could settle down
> If I could settle down
> Then I would settle down

I loved that song. The whole album,
Crooked Rain, Crooked Rain meant a lot to
me. Colette and I'd played it all last summer.
It belonged to us, but I loved it. This surprised
me. I'd thought everything we'd had was
tainted.

Nomi was helping a young businessman pick
out a bong. She waved at me with her fingers.
I'd never seen that kind of wave before. I
laughed.

A dog was sleeping on a piece of carpet
in the corner. I went and stood by the dog. I
decided to walk around the store.

There was fair-trade clothing from around
the world, glass shelves full of glass bongs and
pipes, vegan lotions, vegan incense, even vegan
chapstick.

The young businessman said he'd come
back later, after work, to study the bong situation in more detail.

Nomi said it was time for her lunch break, did I want to go for a walk? Of course. She brought the dog along.

I asked if it was her dog, and she said no, she was just babysitting. I asked what the dog's name was, and she said Rover.

I said Rover was a great name for a dog because it'd been so overused at one time that now it was capable of being used again with vengeance.

She laughed and handed me the leash. I didn't know how to work it. Nothing big, nothing heavy. She showed me how to hold the button to let the dog run, and how to press the button to stop him.

Then she unclipped the leash, and Rover ran ahead, down the busy sidewalk. I didn't like that. I condemned it in my heart. But Nomi was my friend, and I couldn't condemn my friend.

She said, "Rover, come back!"

And Rover came back.

About the Author

Anthony Schlagel grew up pastorally and anachronistically in rural Minnesota. He migrated west with the wagon trains to San Francisco where he studied poetry. To support himself he drove a cab for several years at night. Wearily, he traveled eastward to Tennessee to become a librarian. He lives restively in rural Arizona. More information can be found on his website, *www.anthonyschlagel.com.*

Wet Cement Press Titles

Series 1

My Dog, Me (novel), Anthony Schlagel
ISBN 978-1-7324369-3-0 (2019)

Saraswati's Lament (poetry), Barbara Roether
ISBN 978-1-7324369-0-9 (2019)

Synonym for Home (poetry), *Michelle* Murphy
ISBN 978-1-7324369-2-3 (2019)

Wilson Wiley Variations (poetry), Thoreau Lovell
ISBN 978-1-7324369-1-6 (2019)